KIDS' KLASSICS

NYLA AND THE WHITE CROCODILE

Norma R. Youngberg

Pacific Press®
Publishing Association

Nampa, Idaho | Oshawa, Ontario, Canada
www.pacificpress.com

Designed by Kristin Hansen-Mellish
Cover by Ned Mueller
Illustrated by Thomas Dunbebin

Originally published in 1963.

Copyright © 2013 edition by
Pacific Press® Publishing Association
Printed in the United States of America
All rights reserved

The author assumes full responsibility for the accuracy of all facts and quotations as cited in this book.

You can obtain additional copies of this book by calling toll-free 1-800-765-6955 or by visiting www.adventistbookcenter.com. You can purchase this as an e-book by visiting www.adventist-ebooks.com.

ISBN 13: 978-0-8163-1724-0
ISBN 10: 0-8163-1724-0

December 2013

1

NYLA stood close to the fence that railed in the longhouse veranda and looked down at the river. Everyone in the Dyak village had crowded to the same spot, and a great trembling ran through the company like wind through the thick leaves of a tree.

Yes, Nyla could see in the moonlight a long, pale shape crossing the stream. The water scarcely moved, for the tide was turning. The mighty Tatau River lay under the rising moon, still as a mountain lake.

"Ah-h-h-h!" A tormented sigh rose from all the villagers gathered at the wooden railing. "It comes back again!"

Nyla felt her stomach twist with sick worry. The pale crocodile was coming back. She could hardly bear to look at it, but she must. They had all hoped they would never see such a thing again, but now Nyla couldn't take her eyes from the sleek, glistening form of the white crocodile drawing nearer with every heartbeat. The monstrous creature intended to slither right up the creek under their longhouse just as it had done for the past two nights.

What could such a crocodile want in this small stream? The creek was hardly big enough for it to turn around in, and the water was muddy and dirty from village rubbish and the village pigs. What could any crocodile find attractive here? And who had ever seen a crocodile of such a pale color? The river crocodiles were all dark, almost like the swamp mud that bordered the jungle streams, but this one was tawny, almost white. No one in the village had ever seen it until two nights ago.

Nyla knew that the Tatau River was very wide and many miles long, but no one in all the river villages had ever spoken of such a crocodile. How could it have gotten into the river? Where could it have hidden? How could it have grown to such a size without people's seeing it? It must be many years old.

Now the crocodile had reached the creek's mouth, and with a graceful flip of its tail, slipped into the channel of the smaller stream and lay along the bottom as though it had come to a familiar refuge, a place where it felt at home.

"The Great White One has come again," Chief Ladah announced to his people, and although his voice was loud, it shook a little.

Every person in Ladah's village already knew this visitor had come, and they all answered, "Yes, yes. What shall we do?"

"We must call a council and decide," the chief said. "Malik, you will need your strongest witchcraft. Bring out all your charms."

The witch doctor, Malik, hurried to his room in the longhouse while the women lighted coconut-oil lamps and set them on the floor of the inner veranda. Then the men settled themselves in a circle, and the women and children sat back in the deep shadows beyond the ring of light Nyla, the chief's only daughter, sat with her mother and little brother Djeelee and watched the witch doctor come back with his basket of charms. She listened to all the words the men spoke.

"Chief Ladah," the witch doctor began. "There is a curse on our village. This is no ordinary creature that has come these three nights to our creek. It must be a spirit crocodile, and we shall find out why it comes here and what punishment it intends to bring upon us."

One after another, the village men talked about the evil deeds that had been done in Ladah's village. Almost every man could think of some bad thing his neighbors had done, and a few confessed that they had dreamed bad dreams and done nothing about them. They should have taken down the clusters of heads that hung in front of the village doors and fed them and spoken kind words to them. But rice was scarce this year, and there didn't seem to be enough for feeding the living people.

As the talk ran on, the witch doctor spread his charms in the middle of the circle and prepared to cast lots to find out which family in the village was to blame for this threat of the white crocodile. Malik shook his clusters of bones and polished seeds. He flourished the monkey skull and the small dried crocodile that were his favorite charms. And all the while, he murmured incantations to the spirits, entreating them to point out which family of Ladah's village was to blame.

At last he called out an order to one of the men, who hurried trembling down the notched-log ladder that led from the longhouse veranda to the ground. A squawking of fowls troubled the air for a moment, then the man came springing back up onto the veranda with a long-legged fighting cock in his hand.

With more flourishes of the charms and entreating of the spirits, the witchman swung the chicken around his head, and finally, with a quick, deft movement, he whipped out his belt knife and slashed off the fowl's head. Then, as all the men crowded about, he opened it and examined the liver.

At last he waved his bloody hands over the awed company and said, "The spirits have spoken; the omens are clear. It is Chief Ladah's family who have done the wrong. It is they who are to blame for the pale crocodile's visits. There will be trouble. There will be grief. There will be sorrow."

The witch doctor's final words were almost drowned in a burst of wailing from the women. The chief bowed his head like a man shocked beyond feeling. For a long time he did not speak, and gradually the whole company quieted and sat waiting. The oil lamps flared and smoked. The jungle, just beyond the wide-open front of the longhouse, seemed to crouch in the darkness as though waiting to spring on them. The pale moonlight bathed every object with a deathly glow. Night sounds of innumerable insects buzzed and droned in the warm air, but no one thought of anything but the huge form of the spirit crocodile lying right now in the creek just below their village.

No one questioned the witch doctor's word or his decision. The charms he used were the ones the village folks had trusted for years—as long as any of them could remember. Malik's father had been a witchman before him, and the charms had been handed down from father to son. Malik's mother still lived in the village, a leader in spirit worship.

Nyla felt an agony of fear rise up in her, and when her mother's arm slipped around her she buried her face in her mother's shoulder and sobbed quietly. What could her father have done wrong? There was no one in all the world whom Nyla loved so much as her father. She looked at him now, dressed in his new red loincloth, with his thick black hair twisted into a long knot at the back of his head, while over his eyes the front lock was cut off in a long bang. His head bowed on his chest and his whole body sagged as though with a weight too heavy to support.

Then the chief lifted his head and spoke. "My people, the charms and incantations have discovered the truth. It is indeed my family who have brought this great danger to our village. You all remember that the old chief, my father, many years ago stole a Kayan girl from the upriver people. My father's men took many heads on that trip, but this one girl my father saved because she was so beautiful. He brought her home to this village, and when she was grown he gave her in marriage to Eetop the boaster. Eetop mistreated and neglected her, and one morning we found her dead in the creek below the village." His voice faltered.

Malik took up the story. "Yes, and on that day the old chief died. I remember it well. And on that very day Chief Ladah's daughter Nyla was born."

A murmur of wonder and grief swept the company, and some of the women began to rock back and forth and moan as they always did when they mourned or grieved for the sick or the dead.

Nyla heard her name and sat up straight. A black curtain of terror seemed to shut her out from everyone on the veranda. She had been born on the very day of this terrible happening. What could that mean?

She listened to the witch doctor's voice as he spoke. "Now I will tell you what the charms have said." Malik's small, close-set eyes glittered as he searched the company. Nyla was sure he was looking for her. She crouched lower in the shadows. "The charms have said that the spirit of the Kayan girl lives in this white crocodile. She has come back to the spot where she died, and she comes to punish."

"If we all stay away from the creek, what can the crocodile do?" one of the men asked.

"Stupid one." Malik spit out the words. "This is a spirit crocodile. She has power to bring sickness to the village, to destroy the rice crops, and to bring all kinds of bad luck. She does not always stay in the creek Who knows what she does when she goes out into the open river?"

Every Dyak on the veranda seemed to settle lower in discouragement.

At last Chief Ladah spoke again. "What can we do to turn aside this curse? Can you not make strong medicine and drive the crocodile away?"

Malik's voice scoffed. "You also forget that this is a spirit crocodile. The chief will be required to make a great sacrifice. Since the chief's daughter was born on the day the Kayan girl died, the curse will doubtless fall on her." The witchman's face seemed to brighten. "Yes, we can count it as a certainty. The curse is directed to the chief's daughter."

A scream came up in Nyla's throat and she held her hand over her mouth to stifle it. What could Malik mean?

Chief Ladah sprang to his feet. Nyla had never heard his voice so heavy or so harsh. "I must consider. I must consider. Tomorrow, when the sun is at the zenith we will meet here on this spot to decide what must be done to make medicine against the Great White One." He paused for a moment, his sharp glance on Malik, the witchman. "Go. I, your chief, tell you to go to your rooms at once."

One by one the village folks stole away to their own rooms in the longhouse, but Chief Ladah stood alone where they had left him with his *kris* in his hand. It was a long, sharp, double-bladed weapon that he always carried in a sheath hung at his belt. He fingered the blade and balanced the *kris* in his hand.

Nyla crept up softly and stood beside him. He led her to the veranda railing. The moon rode high in the sky, and a ghostly radiance glowed over the face of the jungle and the river and the little creek below them. The small stream flowed not ten steps from the notched-log ladder that led from the veranda floor down to the ground at the back of the longhouse. The long white shape of the spirit crocodile glistened wet in the moonlight.

Nyla knew what was in her father's mind.

"No, no, my father, who ever heard of one man going out in the night to kill such a crocodile all by himself? No, you must not think of it. This is a spirit crocodile. Your *kris* would certainly have no power against her."

With a deep sigh Chief Ladah thrust the *kris* back into its sheath. "You are right, my daughter, we must think of some other way, some better way. It is not our custom to kill any of the crocodile people unless they first take some of our people. It would not be good to break the custom. It might make more trouble."

Then, as they stood watching, the giant creature turned herself in the narrow creek bed and slipped gracefully out into the mighty Tatau River. The moonbeams picked out her white shape, and they saw her clearly as she turned again in the river current and swam past the village, down the bosom of the river, drifting with the outrunning tide.

"Do you suppose she has a den like other crocodiles?" Nyla asked.

"Who knows?" Chief Ladah groaned. "Who knows? She is a spirit crocodile. There's no telling what she has out in that river."

"It is I who am cursed, isn't it, my father?" Nyla asked. "That's what Malik says."

"What does that mean?" Nyla felt her father's hand tremble even as it clasped her own in a firm, warm grasp. "Does it mean that the crocodile has come for me?"

Ladah looked down at his daughter, and even in the faint moonlight Nyla could see the agony in her father's face. "Nothing shall happen to you, my daughter. Tomorrow we will hold a council and make plans. There must be some way to turn aside this curse. Perhaps the crocodile will not come back again."

Nyla went to her father's room, the first one in the longhouse and nearest to the river. She lay down on her sleeping mat, but sleep would not come. She listened and waited for her father to come in, but there was no sound, no sign. At last she went to the door and peered into the night. A tall figure paced back and forth along the outer rail of the veranda.

Nyla knew that her father was thinking, planning, trying to find some way to deliver the village from the threat of the white crocodile and to save his daughter from the curse of the Kayan girl. Comforted, she went back to her sleeping mat, and late in the night she drowsed off into light slumber.

While Nyla slept she dreamed that she stood on the bank of the little creek with a ball of cooked rice in her hands. Before her, in the moonlight, the great crocodile lay with her nose pointed up the creek toward the jungle.

In her dream Nyla carried the ball of rice and laid it down close to the crocodile's long jaws.

Then the Great White One turned herself across the narrow creek bed. Her stalky eyes seemed to peer at Nyla through the darkness, and they did not look unfriendly. With one gulp the creature swallowed the rice ball and then, turning clear around, she slipped back into the river.

With a gasp of relief the girl wakened and saw the sun peering in her window.

Both father and mother were gone from their sleeping mats, but Djeelee still slept. Outside she heard the women climbing up and down the notched-log ladder with their bamboos filled with fresh water for the morning cooking. Dozens of cocks crowed under the house, and every dog in the village barked as the dogs always did to welcome the new day.

Then the events of last evening rolled across Nyla's mind and crushed all the joy out of her. For the first time in her thirteen years of life, she was sorry that another morning had come.

There were twenty-one doors in Ladah's longhouse, and almost a hundred people lived under that high-pitched roof. She had been born here and she was the chief's daughter, but surely there could not be another person in this village or in all the river villages so wretched as she—cursed from the day of her birth. And no one had guessed such a thing until this awful crocodile came.

2

NYLA sat on the open platform of her jungle village home and pulled strands of split bamboo into the pattern of a shovel-shaped basket for winnowing rice. The girl worked fast because her mind was troubled, and her thoughts flew back and forth like the strips of bamboo she threaded in and out, in and out.

The worry of the white crocodile hung over the entire village like a black cloud. The men had held a secret council this noon, but none of the women or children had been allowed to listen to what they said. After the council Nyla had heard her father and Malik, the witch doctor, arguing. She could remember words that Malik had said. They hung in the air like wasps trying to sting. "It is your daughter, Nyla. She is the one who must go."

Now what could Malik mean? Go where? Would they send her away from mother and father and little brother? Would they sell her to the Chinese? Nyla didn't know; and the more she worried, the faster she pulled the bamboo strips in and out. Her heartbeat pounded in her ears like the thumps of a signal drum. And then she knew the sound was not in her own chest but out in the river.

She ran to the low fence that railed in the veranda's open platform and looked down on the river. Yes, it must be strange paddles beating their way up the stream—not in sight yet, but just around the curve. She watched and waited until the boat appeared at the bend a few hundred yards below Ladah's wharf of floating logs.

"Come, come," she shouted to the women who pounded rice on the open veranda platform and to the children playing there. "It is a boat, a strange boat with only one man in it, and he is wearing clothes."

"Must be a Chinese." Nyla's mother shaded her eyes with one hand and examined the approaching boat. She held Djeelee up to look. "See, it is a Chinese boat, not hollowed out of a log like ours, but made of boards fastened together. See, it is painted white and the paddles are red."

Everyone watched the small white boat swerve in toward the near shore and tie up at their own wharf. They were torn between fear and curiosity. Should they stay to look or should they run? They ran.

They scurried behind baskets and piles of mats or heaps of thatch. All of them hid, but everyone hid where he or she could watch the stranger come up into the longhouse.

Nyla, being the chief's daughter, and already thirteen years old, felt braver than the other village folks. She was more curious than afraid, so she hid close to the notched-log ladder that led up from the bank above the wharf and into the end of the longhouse nearest the river. She ducked behind a big *gusi* jar that Dyaks use for burial purposes. So Nyla got the first look at the young man.

He wore a white sun helmet and was dressed in light-brown shirt and short pants of the same material. His feet and legs were bare, like those of Nyla's people, the Dyaks. His skin was brown too, as brown as her own. He looked like a Dyak with clothes—a most unusual and amusing sight.

The young man's face looked bright and friendly, and he spoke words that Nyla could understand. "Peace be to this house. I have come to visit Chief Ladah and his family."

When no one appeared to welcome him, the man did a terrifying thing. He took a small object from the pocket of his pants and put it to his lips. A piercing sound shattered the still air. It sounded to Nyla like a hornbill, only the sound was a hundred times louder.

The people who had hidden in places where it would be convenient to watch the stranger now decided that they had not chosen well. Everyone scrambled in panic-stricken haste for the dark inner rooms of the longhouse.

Then Chief Ladah appeared at the first door of the village. With his sharp jungle knife in his hand, he faced the young man; but he did not speak.

Nyla could see that her father stood a little taller than the young stranger. The heavy silver ornaments in the lobes of the chief's ears pulled them down until they touched his shoulders. There were no ornaments in the young man's ears, although there were holes that seemed to have partly healed.

The chief looked frightened and a little surprised. Surely no chief in any of the river villages had ever heard such a sound as the young man made with that small thing between his lips.

"I have brought you a gift." The stranger took a step toward Chief Ladah. "I have brought you a voice that will call your people at any time. They can hear it from far down the river."

Again he put the thing to his lips and made the fearful noise. Then he handed the small silvery object to the chief. Ladah took the whistle in his hand. He lifted it to his lips and blew a tremendous blast. People streamed out of the longhouse doors and raced for the ladders. Men who had been mending their nets under the longhouse and those who had been dozing in their rooms came tumbling out, all ready to run to the jungle or the river to escape the strange and fearful noise.

Malik came last. His small black eyes darted this way and that. Nyla could not tell whether he was afraid or curious or angry. It was always hard to tell from Malik's face what was going on in his mind.

Then the strange young man spoke to the chief again. "I am Poojee. I have come to bring you good news about the living God, the God of heaven. I am His messenger."

Again the chief put the whistle to his lips and blew. The people all shrank back, and the chief looked pleased. He motioned them all into a circle on the open veranda. The sun hung low over the northern mountain, now, and the open platform under the sky was the most comfortable spot in the longhouse.

When all the men had settled themselves in the circle and the women and children had filled up the shadowy corners behind them, the chief spoke. "This young man, Poojee, has come to our village to bring us a message, and I have called you together to hear it."

Poojee, who sat by the chief's side, leaned forward. "I am your friend." His voice sounded happy. "I have come to live among you and tell you the good news about the God of heaven, the living God who made the river, the trees, the animals, the sun, moon, and stars, and all the Dyak people."

"Did your God make crocodiles too?" Malik asked.

"Yes, of course He made crocodiles. He made everything, and He is always with us, even though we cannot see Him. His presence is here right this——"

15

At this instant a fresh breeze from the river swept through the veranda—an invisible presence. Every man in the circle around Poojee drew in his breath and let it out in a long "Ah-h-h-h!"

Shivers ran up Nyla's spine into her hair. She knew that this strange young teacher was making powerful magic.

The unexpected breeze passed by. Everything grew still, and Chief Ladah leaned forward. "We are having trouble with crocodiles, great trouble."

Malik put out his hand in a gesture of impatience. "What can this strange youth know about our crocodile trouble? Who knows? Perhaps he is the first of the curses the white crocodile brings to this village." He spat a mouthful of betel-nut juice on the bamboo floor.

Chief Ladah looked sharply at the witchman. "Perhaps this stranger's God is a stronger witch doctor than you are. Maybe He knows ways to handle crocodiles that you have never thought of."

Malik did not answer, but his face darkened with anger.

"Would you like to tell me about your trouble?" Poojee waited.

The chief frowned at Malik, rolled himself another wad of betel nut, and then began his story about the mysterious white crocodile that had come for three evenings to the little creek below the village. He told the story of the Kayan girl. "You see," he finished, "there is indeed a heavy curse upon our longhouse. We know that now."

Malik moved closer to the teacher. His small eyes glittered and his lips drew away from his sharp, yellow teeth. "Yes, there is a curse upon all of us, and it is the chief's family who brought it here. The chief knows what he must do."

The witch doctor sprang to his feet, rushed over and seized Nyla, and dragged her into the circle, holding her out for the teacher to see. "This is the girl the white crocodile is after. This is the chief's daughter."

Nyla twisted in Malik's grasp, and screams came up in her throat. She tried to hold them back, but a few came out. Then Nyla's mother came and took her from the witch doctor's hands and drew her back into the shadows outside the circle.

"But, no," the teacher was saying, "the girl is not to blame. She did not choose the day she should be born. It is not her fault that her grandfather was a cruel man."

"There, you see?" Malik's face was black with anger. "This stranger can do nothing to help us. Let us not be fooled by his talk about an unseen God. Let us put an end to this foolishness at once."

Chief Ladah raised his hand and quieted the people, for some of them had already raised their voices in agreement with Malik. "It is since the white crocodile came that we are sure of this curse. The Kayan girl's spirit lives in the crocodile and that is why she keeps coming back. No other crocodile has ever come into our creek."

Then Poojee raised his voice so everyone could hear. "My God is very great. My God is greater than all the crocodiles and all the curses in the world. He is always with us. He is here right now, and we must not be afraid."

Then the teacher began to sing in a sweet, low voice, but every Dyak on the longhouse veranda could understand the words of his song:

> "Within the mighty love of God,
> I am safe, always safe.

Nothing hurts or frightens me;
I am safe, always safe.
Winds and water roar and rage;
I am safe, always safe.
God is with me everywhere;
I am safe, always safe."

As the song ended, the chief stood up, and everyone on the veranda jumped up and moved silently to the railing and looked down into the river. Nyla stood close to her mother. She still trembled with fear, and her throat ached with the crying she tried to hold back.

There below them in the river they could all see the enormous white crocodile swimming slowly upstream in front of their floating log wharf. The creature turned toward the creek's mouth and slipped gracefully into the shallow water of the little stream.

Great fear shook the whole company, and a moan of terror went up as one voice from them all. Only the teacher, Poojee, leaned with calm and controlled attention on the veranda railing.

"Look," the chief pointed. "She comes again." His voice was a shaken whisper. Nyla could see that her father and all the other villagers now looked upon the crocodile as the embodiment of the Kayan girl—not just an ordinary female crocodile of the rivers.

"What a strange color for a crocodile," Poojee said. "I have never seen such a light-skinned one before. But how do you know she is dangerous? Most crocodiles are quite harmless, you know."

Then all the pent-up fury of the past three days flared up and burst in Malik. He screamed. He raged. He danced in a frenzy of excitement. "Go!" he commanded the teacher. "Go now. Leave this village. We want no more of your talk or your magic. Chief Ladah knows what he must do. You are only delaying him. Be gone!"

As Malik screamed out his fierce words he pushed the teacher toward the edge of the platform where the notched-log ladder led down to the riverbank.

Chief Ladah did not speak. Like a man in a dream, he stood watching that long white shape resting in the creek below the village.

The teacher glanced around at all the people with a kind look, but he did not resist Malik. He allowed himself to be pushed to the edge of the veranda and he went down the notched-log ladder without looking back. He untied his white boat, and the whole company saw him pull off upriver with steady rhythmic strokes of his paddle. Behind the boat a wake of shimmering water glistened and faded. Then they heard the rower's voice raised in song:

"Go!" Malik commanded the teacher. "Go now! Leave this village. We want no more of your talk of magic."

> "Within the mighty love of God,
> I am safe, always safe…"

Malik called all the men back into the circle where they had been sitting before they ran to the railing to look for the crocodile.

"You know what you must do." The witch doctor spoke to the chief. "You must send your daughter to make peace with the crocodile. There is no other way."

Terror struck at Nyla like a snake in the dark. She could scarcely believe the words. What could they mean? Must she go alone to meet the crocodile? What would happen then?

She looked at her father. He had come to sit in the circle of men, but his head was still bowed and his eyes appeared to see nothing. Could he hear and understand what Malik was saying? Her mind ran in a whirl of fear, like a small animal trapped in a cage, round and round. Then a clear sweet sound cut through her thoughts, clear as a blade of light—the words of Poojee's song:

> "Within the mighty love of God,
> I am safe, always safe…"

She remembered her dream. Yes, she must go and make a peace offering to the spirit crocodile. She ran to her father's side.

"Look, my father, do not be afraid. I will go and make peace with the Great White One. I will go now."

"No, no." The chief grabbed both her hands. "No, my daughter. You will become the offering. The dreadful creature has come to get you. Don't go. There must be some other way!"

"I must go," Nyla insisted. "I am the only one who can turn aside the curse."

Malik and some of the other village men loosened the chief's hands. "Are you the chief of the village and refuse to allow your daughter to make the sacrifice to protect your people?" Malik threw his powerful arms around the chief.

"How do you know that the teacher could not have helped us? Why did you drive him away?" The chief's voice was loud and angry, but his friends held him fast.

Nyla slipped into her mother's kitchen. She felt in the dark for the rice kettle. Yes, there was rice left in it. She scraped it out and made a ball of it, as much as she could carry in her two hands.

Where could mother be? Then Nyla knew. Malik had seen to it that neither of her parents would prevent her going to the crocodile with her offering.

3

MEEKLY obeying the witch doctor's orders, Nyla climbed down the longhouse ladder to make an offering of rice to the white crocodile. Slowly she walked to the bank of the creek.

Just a few steps away from her she could see the huge form of the white crocodile in the shallow stream. Only the melody of Poojee's song ringing in her mind and the memory of last night's dream held her there on the creek bank.

She looked up to the longhouse veranda above her and saw that all the village people had gathered to watch. She could feel their held breath, the agony of their waiting. She urged her trembling feet forward and held out the ball of rice with both hands. The clear moonlight shimmered along the whole length of the crocodile's wet back and glistened on the scaly surface. The Great White One was bigger than she had realized.

As the girl waited, the monster form in the creek turned with a mighty slap of her tail and lay across the channel of the stream facing her. It was almost more than Nyla could endure to face that savage, long-jawed look. She laid the rice ball in front of the crocodile's wicked nose.

The stalky eyes seemed to turn toward the girl; then with one gulp, the creature swallowed the rice ball. As though satisfied, the enormous crocodile writhed and turned her bulk until she faced the mouth of the creek and slithered out into the main current of Tatau River. With deliberate majesty, the mighty creature swam on the river's surface, down toward the curve of the stream below Ladah's village.

For a moment Nyla stood on the spot where she had faced the crocodile. Relief flooded through her whole body, for she had come with a peace offering and the Great White One had accepted it and gone away. Now perhaps the trouble would be ended. What more could the crocodile want?

She climbed the notched-log ladder with light steps and felt her mother's arms around her and her father's voice saying, "My daughter, you are a brave girl."

"It was the song," Nyla exclaimed, "the song the strange teacher brought. I remembered the words:

" 'God is with me everywhere;
I am safe, always safe.' "

Then Nyla saw Malik. His face was twisted with anger and hate. Deep inside, the girl knew that the witch doctor was not satisfied. No offering that might pacify the crocodile would suit Malik unless it cost her own life.

In spite of Malik's black looks, Nyla slept well that night. After her terrible experience on the creek bank, she no longer feared the white crocodile. She felt sure that the huge beast was not a killer, but one of the indifferent creatures that swam about the village wharf every day—the ordinary river crocodiles. Her color made people notice her and fear her, but underneath that light, scaly hide, she was certainly no different from the other crocodile people.

One matter troubled Nyla. What would Malik do now?

23

What if the crocodile should come back this evening? Would Malik make her go with another offering? She knew that the witch doctor had been disappointed last night when she took the peace offering and suffered no harm.

Then her thoughts flew to the young teacher, Poojee, whom the witch doctor had driven away from their village. Where was he now? Had some of the upriver villages welcomed him? If they hadn't, where could he have gone?

She ran out into the open veranda and found her mother pounding rice. "Mother, why did Malik send that teacher away? I liked him and I liked his song."

Mother looked at her sharply. "You heard what Malik said. I have never seen him so angry."

"But why, Mother?" Nyla asked. "The teacher spoke good words. They made me feel warm inside and not afraid."

"Yes, I felt the same way myself, but you see, that's just the trouble. Malik saw that the teacher was making powerful magic. He was catching the people's hearts. Malik is frightened."

"Then there really is a God we cannot see?" "The men don't know. They are afraid." "Did my father keep the small thing that makes the sharp noise?"

"He kept it." Nyla thought mother's voice sounded troubled.

"Mother, if it should be true?" Nyla hesitated. "If there really is a God we cannot see—then maybe——"

"Don't speak of it. I am frightened too." Mother spoke in a low whisper and drew the girl back into their own room of the longhouse. "You are not to worry. Your father will never let Malik hurt you."

"But Malik had his way about the teacher. It was Malik

who drove him away. My father liked Poojee. And Malik made my father let me go alone to make the offering to the crocodile last night. Is Malik stronger?"

Then mother gathered Nyla into her arms, and they both cried softly in the shadowed inner room.

Nyla controlled herself at last. "Why does Malik hate me so?" she asked.

Mother thought for a long time. "I think the main reason is that your father loves you so much. Malik would like your father to make him first in everything." Mother hesitated. "Malik is jealous of you. He doesn't think it is right for a chief to make his daughter first in everything."

"But Malik is first in his mother's eyes."

"Yes, I know, but he is a man. That's different. Of course, I do think that Malik believes that the curse of the Kayan girl is on you."

Then they both sat clinging to each other for several minutes. At last Nyla spoke again. "Did you hear that teacher say that his God is stronger than all the crocodiles and all the curses in the world? Do you suppose God is stronger than Malik?"

"I hope so. I hope so. I hope He is stronger than all of us. Oh, I would give God anything if He could break this curse."

Then mother smiled through her tears. "Look, my daughter, it is a beautiful day. Go and play with the other children and forget about the Kayan girl's curse. Since you made the peace offering, perhaps the crocodile will never come back any more."

The sun had just risen, and a cool sweetness filled the air. Of all times of day, Nyla liked the early morning best, with the big sun overhead and the river shining while the jungle birds warbled and monkeys chattered among the trees. Everything seemed safe and pleasant. Nyla could almost forget the trouble hanging over Ladah's village.

With the other village children, she ran down to the riverbank, on the other side of the creek's shallow mouth, where a wide sandbank jutted out into the river. They played a game of twig-tag. One of the children took a twig between his teeth and dived down to the sandy bottom of the river and planted the twig. The others tried to find it. One after another, they planted the twig and brought it up again to the surface. Shouts and laughter rang as the children made merry on the shelving sandbank below Ladah's village.

Nyla was quick as any of them, and she had just come up with the twig in her mouth when a deep rumbling noise arose from the river. A huge form seemed to shimmer just below the water's surface, and a thrashing and struggling filled the stream. Every child streaked out of the water and scrambled in panic-stricken haste up the ladder and into the longhouse.

Chief Ladah ran toward them with his hand on his *kris*.

"What was it, Father? What was it?" Nyla seized her father's hand. Out of breath and shaking with fright, she clung to him. "We were playing over on the sand bar where we always do, and some great big thing came and tumbled and rumbled."

The group of dripping children stood trembling, and they joined their shrill voices to tell a confused story of an enormous crocodile that had risen in the water off the sand bar.

Chief Ladah counted the children to make sure none were missing. Then he chewed his betel nut for several minutes. All the village people had run together, and stood now grouped around the shivering, chattering youngsters. A look of grave concern spread over the chief's handsome face.

Malik came out now, and Nyla looked at him. The witch doctor's face was set in a mask of grim determination. He had made up his mind about something. Nyla was sure of that. The chief looked twice at Malik as though he waited for some word from him, but Malik didn't speak. He pointed down at the sandbank where the children had been playing not five minutes ago. *The sand bar was gone!* The vine-choked bank of the river rose right out of the deep water.

Every person in the village shook with fright. It was as though, by pointing his finger, the witch doctor had blotted the sandbank out of existence. Not a person in Ladah's village doubted that the curse of the Kayan girl must somehow have caused the sandbank to disappear. Such a happening could portend only evil.

The chief and Malik quieted the people and gathered them under the overhanging roof of the inner veranda, for the sun now beat down with fierce heat.

Malik spoke first. "People of Ladah's village, listen to me. You have all seen what happened this morning. Can any of you doubt that the spirit crocodile has done this? Can any of you doubt that the Great White One came to take one of the children?"

Nyla felt the witchman's eyes upon her and knew that he was disappointed again because she had escaped. The day that had begun with hope darkened now with despair. Tonight the white crocodile would come again to the creek, and what would happen then?

The chief looked around at his people. "In all my life," he began, "I have seen a sand bar disappear only once before today."

"Was it because of a curse?" one of the village men asked.

"Perhaps it was. We could not tell. We had dragged a heavy boat up on the bar, and it broke away like a shelf broken from the wall of a room."

"It was the work of evil spirits, no question about that." Malik sat close to the chief and chewed on his cud of betel nut. "What else could it have been?"

The chief didn't seem to hear Malik. He went on talking. "We made a great spirit feast, and no bad luck came to us."

"A feast! A feast!" Voices took up the word and passed it around the circle. There was hope in the word, something to do, something to look forward to, some promise to lift their spirits.

"Yes." The chief looked happier as he went on talking. "I think we should make a great feast, the biggest and best that any chief has ever made on this river. Then perhaps the evil spirit that lives in the white crocodile will go away and leave us alone."

The people in the village wiped the worried frowns from their faces and began to smile and laugh together. Feasts were few on the river, and they were exciting times when everyone ate, drank, and rejoiced. Who would not be glad at such a prospect?

At spirit feasts the dried and smoked heads that hung in clusters in front of every door in the village were taken down, fed with the choicest food, and drenched with rice wine. Such a feast was a safeguard against many troubles—bad dreams, evil omens, accidents, sickness, and poor crops; for the people believed that evil spirits controlled all these misfortunes.

Fear, which had all but paralyzed the people of Ladah's village an hour ago, vanished now in excited talk about the feast.

Even Malik seemed to throw off his sulkiness and join in the plans.

"How many of you are willing to leave your own work and give all your time to getting ready for the feast?" the chief asked.

Not one person held back. Everyone was willing, glad, enthusiastic. Nyla saw that her father's face looked pleasant as it had before the crocodile came.

"You young fellows." The chief pointed to six young men who lolled on the edge of the council circle. "Go downriver and borrow chickens. Borrow all you can, better take three boats. Get back as soon as you can, and wherever you go, spread the news about the feast."

Malik looked at the aged men who sat in honored places in the group. "It is for you old ones to beat the drums and let the whole river know that the chief of Ladah's village prepares the greatest feast the river has ever seen."

"I will lead a fishing party." The chief spoke brightly now. "We will go up the river to a suitable spot and catch enough fish for the feast. You women, prepare the tuba root at once."

Encouraged by talk of the great spirit feast and busy with preparations, all the people felt better. Even Nyla helped her mother gather tuba root and pile it in their boat ready for the fishing expedition that would set out in the morning. The tuba fishing was sure to be successful if a new branch of the river was invaded—one where no tuba had been used for several years. The tuba root produced a paralyzing poison that stupefied the fish and made them easy to catch.

Now the village came alive. People ran here and there. Men loosened their dugouts and hurried up and down the river to neighboring villages on errands. The old men got busy with

In the flash of the eyelash one of the canoes capsized, and a man and woman were thrown into the stream. With a chill of horror Nyla realized that the boat had not turned over by itself.

the drums, and the steady beat of their deep tones throbbed through the still, hot air. Lively chatter filled the longhouse. The thump-thump-thump of women beating out rice, and the laughter of children sounded everywhere. Nyla had almost forgotten the cause of all this activity—the threat of the white crocodile and the curse of the Kayan girl.

The sun was not yet gone from the great river, but its last beams slanted through the tall jungle trees along the banks. From both upriver and downstream, boats were returning filled with tuba root for tomorrow's fishing. Nyla stood at the veranda railing watching them. She wondered whether any of the boats would go far enough upriver to hear news of the teacher—the young man Poojee, whom Malik had driven away from the village.

Even as Nyla watched the busy traffic in the river, an accident happened. It happened so suddenly that even the girl's sharp eyes could not see what caused the trouble. In a flash of the eyelash one of the canoes capsized. The passengers, a man and a woman, were thrown into the stream and disappeared with a great cry. Nyla knew them both. They lived in Ladah's village. They had been out gathering the tuba root.

With a chill of horror, Nyla realized that the boat had not turned over by itself. A huge crocodile must have seen the approaching boat and, timing its action to the dugout's swift motion, reared its heavy body out of the water directly beneath it, overturning the craft and tossing the helpless occupants into the stream.

4

AS Nyla watched, she saw the man and woman who had been knocked out of their canoe struggle to the surface of the river. The crocodile seized the woman by the shoulder and began to sink away toward the bottom, but the woman's husband fastened himself to the crocodile's head and drove both his sharp thumbs into the creature's eyes.

A minute passed. The fierce crocodile still held its struggling victim. Another minute passed. Nyla heard terrible screams coming from somewhere and realized that the screams were her own voice. She was shrieking her loudest, along with several of the women who had joined her at the railing of the veranda.

All through Ladah's village, people shouted and ran this way and that. The men who had been mending nets on the open veranda scrambled down the notched-log ladder to loosen their dugouts.

With mighty thrashings of its tail, the crocodile tried to throw off the man hanging onto its nose, but he was beyond reach of that deadly weapon. Every second the man's thumbs dug deeper into the monster's eyes. Nyla looked down on the struggle from the veranda, fully fifteen feet above the river bank, and thirty feet above the water, but she knew that all the men in the boats could see the fight almost as well as she could.

The sudden twilight had dropped, and all objects in the river held a queer unearthly distinctness without being clearly visible.

With mighty screams, the Dyak men raced the canoes toward the battle. Then the crocodile gave the woman a fierce shake and let her go. The man loosened himself from the monster's head and pushed his wife's unconscious form ahead of him to one of the waiting boats. Gentle hands drew her aboard and tried to stanch the flow of blood from her mangled shoulder.

"Adoh! Adoh! Adohee!" The wailing women's voices rose and fell to the rhythm of the paddles as the boats returned to Ladah's wharf. The whole village was so overwrought with excitement and grief that no one said much. The moaning and wailing expressed far better than any words the sympathy all of them felt for the wounded woman and her brave husband.

The woman lay pale and still in her husband's arms. He carried her up the notched-log ladder and into their own room in the longhouse. There he laid her tenderly on her sleeping mat. The shoulder was swelling now and bleeding less. Malik hurried to prepare a plaster of crushed leaves, which he pressed all around the jagged wound.

The young man, exhausted by his struggle with the killer crocodile, slumped on the mat at his wife's side. Everyone tried to crowd into the room, but Chief Ladah persuaded them to squat on the inner veranda, just outside the door. There they set up a rhythmic wailing that made the falling darkness hideous. It seemed a dark night to Nyla. The moon had not yet risen, and the threat of evil that hung in the air made the night darker than night usually is.

Chief Ladah sat inside the sick woman's room and right

beside the door, where everyone outside could see him. He chewed on his betel nut and waited.

At last he raised his hand to quiet the wailing and spoke. "The curse has fallen, so soon, so soon."

Ladah rocked back and forth as he always did when grieved or excited. His voice was husky and low like a chant. "What shall we do now? Speak up, Malik. What do you say?"

Malik was preparing a fresh poultice for the woman's wounded shoulder. He looked up with a fierce light in his eyes. "The chief knows whom the crocodile is seeking. The chief knows what remedy is needed."

Ladah's eyes seemed to search the assembled people until his look rested on his daughter, and it stayed there a moment.

An expression of agony crossed his face. "My people, we have not yet made the spirit feast. We will continue with all our plans. It will be the greatest feast the river villages have ever seen. Perhaps, even now, the spirit of the Kayan girl will be satisfied and leave."

As Chief Ladah spoke, his voice grew stronger, and he spoke with more authority. "We will all continue with our appointed tasks. Tomorrow you young men will go to borrow the chickens, and I will lead the fishing party up the river. The women will prepare rice cakes. Malik will stay here to care for the wounded woman, and he will perform all the necessary incantations and sacrifices that must come before the feast."

The whole company grunted approval. Everyone felt better now. Even Malik hurried about his duties like a man who has boundless authority and satisfaction.

Nyla had taken an active part in all the excitement of the evening. Now she sat with her mother and her little brother, Djeelee. The tumult in her heart was almost more than she could bear. There was one dreadful question that had not come up yet. She waited for it.

It came now; Malik asked it. "What color was the crocodile that tipped over your boat?" He spoke to the young man whose wife had been mauled by the crocodile.

The man answered in a tired voice. "I don't know. I wasn't thinking about anything but the crocodile's eyes and its sharp teeth that were tearing my wife's shoulder."

Malik stood in the door of the sickroom and called out, "Did any of you see what color that crocodile was?"

No one seemed to know for sure. The terrible accident had happened just at dusk. Only the crocodile's nose was above water. How could they tell? An argument broke out among the men; some said it was the Great White One, but others were sure it wasn't. No one doubted that the Kayan girl's curse was to blame for this new calamity.

That night Nyla was so excited and troubled that sleep would not come to her. She lay on her mat and listened for any unusual sounds or any whispered conversation. The only sounds she heard were the barking of village dogs, the crowing of roosters, and the opening and closing of the door that led into the room where the sick woman lay. Nyla knew that her father would keep watch with Malik and the sick woman's husband all through the night.

Morning came, and the wounded woman appeared to be no worse. All the people in the village felt better. Chief Ladah and his family took a quiet dip in the river, for a morning bath was something no Dyak could do without. They did not linger long in the water; important business hurried them.

"Come, Nyla. Come, Djeelee." The chief wound his long hair, coiled it into a long tight knot at the back of his head, and shook the water from his glistening skin. "Come, we will go now."

Nyla shook out her own long hair, twisted it, and fastened it with a thorn. Djeelee didn't do anything with his hair. He let the wet strands straggle down his naked back. Both children climbed into the dugout, where their mother already sat with the guide paddle in her hand.

"Are we going to need all this tuba to do our fishing?" Nyla kicked at the large bundle of roots stacked in the center of the canoe as she made a place for herself in front of her father.

"We will need more than this." Chief Ladah bent to his paddle with strong arms. "See, every canoe has a big bundle of tuba root. We intend to catch a lot of fish. Remember, this feast is going to be the biggest and best this river has ever seen."

Nyla looked at the boats that followed them. All were stacked with the tuba root, and all were fighting the swift current.

It seemed as though they had been rowing for hours. Mother brought out a couple of palm-leaf hats for the children. These shaded their eyes from the merciless light. The river water was cool, and they dipped their hands in it constantly, often scooping it up to drink.

At midday they loitered in the shade of an overhanging tree and ate their simple meal of rice balls wrapped in banana leaves. Nyla did not feel hungry. She toyed with her rice ball for a moment, then dropped it into the water and watched it sink lower and lower down in the murky depths. Her father looked at her with troubled eyes. Could he know that she was thinking of the rice ball she had fed the crocodile?

Nyla hung over the side of the dugout and a big tear

dropped from the end of her nose into the river, but she dared not cry. Perhaps everything would come out all right after all. Maybe the white crocodile would never come back to their creek again. It hadn't come last night. Maybe the Kayan girl's spirit would be glad for the feast, and everyone in Ladah's village could be happy once more.

As they passed the first of the upriver villages, Nyla remembered Poojee, the teacher. Where was he? She was sure he had not come down the river; someone would have seen him. Why was it no drums had sent any message about him? Was it because the villages were ashamed of his being around and were afraid to beat out such a message on the drums? Then the words of the teacher's song came back to her:

> "God is with me everywhere;
> I am safe, always safe."

That evening they camped on the bank of the big river. The men built a crude shelter of leaves and branches. The women struck fire from their flint stones and made a bright blaze where they boiled pots of rice. In spite of mosquitoes, everyone was tired enough so they slept well.

"Just as I thought," Chief Ladah said the next morning when the sun had risen. "Just as I thought, we are right here at the mouth of the stream where we are going to fish. I recognize that big dead tree standing over on the far bank."

Nyla looked across the Tatau River. It didn't look more than half as wide here as it did beside their own village.

"Djeelee, Djeelee, wake up quick." Nyla shook her brother awake. "The men are already going with the tuba. Wake up, wake up."

Still rubbing his sleepy eyes, Djeelee stumbled to his feet, and Nyla hustled him into the dugout. Mother and the other women had spread out tuba roots on a big flat rock at the mouth of the small stream. Now they beat and bruised the roots with clubs of hard wood or flat stones. The bruised roots gave off a strange odor, and milky juice gathered and clotted over them.

As fast as the pile of bruised tuba roots grew large, one of the men picked it up and took it up the small tributary. The rest of the company spread their dugouts across the river in a loose chain not far from where the creek joined the big river.

In each canoe a Dyak stood with poised spear. Nyla and Djeelee stood in their canoe and watched with excited interest. Djeelee held his own small spear and leaned far out over the water. His black eyes glittered.

"They come, they come!" Nyla screamed, but she did not move. Down the stream, floating toward them, came fish of all sizes. Some floundered weakly, but most of them appeared dead, their white bellies turned up to the morning sun.

The Dyaks thrust here and there, spearing the choicest and largest of the fish. Djeelee stabbed as many as possible and threw them into the boat. Nyla became so excited that she began grabbing the fish out of the water with her hands and cutting them with a sharp knife; for she knew that most of the fish were not actually dead, but only stupefied by the tuba. They would come to life again in a few minutes.

When all the tuba had been used, then the run of fish would be over and there would be no more fishing in this stream for a long time to come.

"Get that big one!" someone yelled. "Catch those two over there! Here, here, help! Push over, push over!" The excited shouting kept on for a full hour. Then with weary arms and legs the men threw themselves down on the riverbank and rested a little.

Ladah had his wish—the dugouts were loaded with fish. No such fishing had taken place for years on the upper Tatau. Surely the omens were good for the coming feast. It was bound to be the grandest the river villages had ever seen. It looked as though the spirits were already pleased. Nyla felt her heavy heart lift. The danger of the Kayan girl's curse might be turned aside. The fleet of fishing canoes made the return trip down the river in half the time it had taken to come up, for they traveled with the current and the outrunning tide. Only one important event occurred. At the log wharf of Sidang village, Nyla saw the white boat that she knew belonged to the teacher, Poojee.

"Look, Father, look, Mother," she cried out. "The teacher is at Sidang village. He must be staying here now."

Chief Ladah gazed at the white boat and then lifted his

The Dyaks thrust here and there, spearing the choicest and largest fish. Nyla grabbed fish with her hands.

eyes to the high veranda of Chief Sidang's longhouse. "Yes, I suppose old Chief Sidang took that teacher in and let him stay. Sidang went on a trip to Singapore years ago, and he has been different ever since."

"Why, Father?" Nyla kept her eyes on the teacher's boat. "Why would going to Singapore make him different?"

"Oh, I suppose he saw a lot of people, a lot of strangers, and now he is not afraid of strangers like Malik and—"

"I wish Poojee had come to stay in our village," Nyla said.

"Yes, I would have liked that myself." Chief Ladah rowed strongly, and now the dugout was rounding a curve that shut Sidang's village from their sight. "Yes, I would have liked to know more about Poojee's teaching, but Malik would have made too much trouble."

Nyla wondered whether Malik was always to have his way by making such savage trouble that no one could stand against him. Somehow the day seemed to darken, and even the huge catch of fish and the good omens for the coming feast didn't comfort her.

By midafternoon, the returning fishing party swept round the bend above Ladah's village, and they began to chant a loud shrill cry of victory, half song, half laughter.

The folks who had stayed home had shown their confidence in the expedition by preparing a large number of bamboo joints. Into these the fish were thrust without much salt, for salt was scarce and precious. The fish had lain for hours in the hot sun. No effort was made to clean them. They had been caught in clean water, hadn't they?

No one was surprised to find that the wounded woman was improving. She was conscious again. The pain in her shoulder was severe, but Malik promised that, with the soothing leaf compresses he had made, she would feel much better in a few more days, although her arm might always be lame.

It seemed to all the villagers that the evil spirits so active earlier in the week had now retreated, and the more kindly spirits were taking a hand in the longhouse affairs.

That evening Nyla's mother explained to her that she would be expected to take a special part in the coming feast. "It is your father's wish. You are thirteen years old, and it will be a great honor for your father to have his own beautiful daughter serve the wine at his door."

"What shall I wear?"

"You may wear all my jewelry and my brass rings. I am sure they will fit you perfectly and you will look lovely. It is all decided."

That night Nyla tried to keep awake to think about the coming feast, but the long trip to the fishing creek had been too tiring. She quickly fell into a sound sleep.

5

THE morning after the fishing trip Nyla stood on the open veranda of the longhouse and saw that full jars of rice wine had been set by each of the twenty-one doors in the longhouse. The jars stood tall, almost as tall as little brother Djeelee. The wine was good. She had seen the women make it. It took hours and hours of chewing the raw rice for each jar. For days afterward the women would complain of aching jaws.

The feast preparations lacked only the chickens. And where could the chickens be?

Chief Ladah worried aloud. "Those fellows must have gone clear down past the Fort. Maybe they even went to the Malay village at the river's mouth. How can it take them so long? The feast is only three days away."

The chief ordered the drummers to ask for news of the three boats that had set out from his village to borrow chickens for the great feast. Word came back, by way of the drums, that the young men were almost home, that their trip had been successful, and that all three dugouts appeared to be loaded with chickens.

The women sharpened their knives and waited. Nyla thought about the drums and the news they had brought. Was it not a good omen? All the people in the river villages wanted to help with the feast, otherwise they would not have loaned chickens. Of course, everyone knew that at future feasts they would borrow back what fowls they needed.

The boats came in that evening. A shrill squawking of chickens announced their arrival. Every person in the village ran down to the log wharf. The three dugouts tied up alongside, each loaded with long-legged fowls. All hands grappled with the chicken baskets and lugged them up into the longhouse, where the chickens were set, still in their basket cages, to wait for the morning.

Early the next morning Nyla was on hand to watch the women at their final task. They killed the fowls one by one and stripped off most of the feathers. They pounded the chicken carcasses between two heavy stones until the flesh was beaten to rags, then they dropped the raw flesh into the jars of rice wine.

"Why don't you take the insides out of them?" Djeelee asked his mother.

"Foolish little boy," his mother answered. "Don't you know that a Dyak's stomach never keeps anything he eats at a feast? Why should we go to all that work?"

As Nyla watched the finishing touches being put on the preparation for the feast, her heart lifted and gladness made her feel like dancing around the working women and the jars of rice wine. Tomorrow the feast would begin, and dressed in her mother's beautiful jewelry, she would serve wine at her father's door.

Beside the wine jars stood bamboo joints full of the fish they had caught five days ago. The odor from their contents filled the air. Even to the middle of the river one could smell it, and no one passing by, out in the stream, could help knowing what preparations were in progress for Ladah's feast.

Nyla could hardly wait. The peaceful day, the busy women, the sheen of sunlight on the river, the delicious food and drink waiting, all these added to her hope that the omens were good. Best of all, the wounded woman was getting better, and the white crocodile had not come back to their creek since the night the woman was hurt.

That night Nyla fell asleep and did not waken until the feast-day sun stood bright and shining, flooding the river with sunlight.

As on every other day, the first task was the early morning bath. Then, fresh from her dip in the river, Nyla stood still while her mother arranged her belt, fashioned from many brass wires and hung with coins of gold and silver. Mother adjusted the belt until it exactly fitted the girl's slender waist.

"You must look beautiful on this day," mother said as she worked to get the belt just right. "Remember, you are the only daughter of Chief Ladah, and you must do him honor."

The leg bands of brass rings came next, then the arm bands, and last of all the heavy necklaces of old and precious beads. On her head, Nyla wore a high crown fashioned of white orchids. She felt weighted down with it all, but proud and important.

"Do I look all right?" She turned to her mother.

"You are lovely as the river at sunrise." Chief Ladah's voice broke in on them. "No other chief in all the river villages has so fair a daughter." He patted Nyla's cheek. "See, the canoes are already coming." He pointed through the open door, out toward the river.

Nyla walked to the end of the longhouse veranda, where she could look down on the river. From far upstream, from down the river as far as the great curve, came the dugout canoes. Painted and plumed in gaudy splendor, the warriors pulled toward Ladah's village. They shouted and sang. They contorted their bodies in wild merriment, for this feast was to be the greatest the river had ever seen, a spirit feast, their highest duty and supreme pleasure.

Nyla took up her station beside the jar of wine at her father's door, the first one in the longhouse and nearest to the river. In her hands she held the skull of a large monkey ingeniously fashioned into a cup holding a pint or more. She dipped it into the jar and stood waiting with the brimming cup in her hands.

"Spirits of the river!" cried Chief Sidang. "What have we here? A very fair daughter indeed. Chief Ladah, I trust that your wine is as pleasant to the lips as your daughter is to the eyes."

Nyla flushed with pleasure as she watched Sidang empty the cup.

After he had accepted and downed the offering of wine, he knelt beside the wine jar while Nyla's mother graciously dredged up rags of chicken for him, as well as drips and draggles of the well-ripened fish together with rice cakes. Then Chief Sidang moved on to the next door of the longhouse, where another fair daughter waited to repeat the offering with a coconut full of wine.

It was the wine that made the feast. At every one of the twenty-one doors in Ladah's longhouse, one of the village women waited to extend hospitality to the guests. Each tried to overwhelm the visitors with generosity, and not one guest among them was so ill-mannered as to refuse either wine or food; although, after the first few doors, the guest was obliged to go over to the railing and disgorge the cargo he had already taken aboard, in order to take in more. Later, down toward the end of the row of doors, most of the guests were not able to reach the railing, and some of them did not try.

Nyla stayed at her post until a hundred or more guests had been served. This was her first appearance at a feast, and she intended to do her full duty. True, there had been other feasts on the river and even in Ladah's village, but only the men ate and drank; no children had been allowed. The women prepared the food and wine, but they served it to the men and looked on without partaking.

Ladah traded polite words with his guests for a while, taking great pride in the compliments showered on his beautiful daughter; but as the feast progressed, he drank more and more, until he, as well as most of the guests, was helplessly drunk.

Some of the men wanted to fight, others were hilarious, many were simply unconscious. A few of the less important men in the village had been charged by Chief Ladah with keeping order. They were forbidden to drink under threat of severe punishment by the spirits in whose honor the feast was being held.

Malik had instructed these men to take down the clusters of heads from the rafters of the veranda ceiling and feed them with fish and chicken and rice cakes. This they did, with reverent attention. And as they fed the heads and poured wine between the grinning teeth, they spoke many kind words to each of the heads so that the spirits of the persons who formerly owned the heads might be comforted and prevented from sending bad dreams into the village or doing other mischief.

These heads had been collected in years gone by. Time was when every warrior in all the Dyak villages had several heads to his credit, and the notches on his *kris* handle proved it. Now the British overlords frowned on headhunting. It must be done in secret and with dangers unknown in the old days. Everyone believed that unless the heads were well treated they might cause a lot of trouble in the village. Evil omens dogged the trail of any man who disregarded the heads and their spirits.

Chief Ladah was indulgent; he had provided magnificently for the heads. As Nyla watched the feeding of the heads she thought that no spirit would have any cause for complaint.

As soon as a man became helplessly drunk or too eager to fight, the village police whom Ladah had appointed fastened the man's hands behind his back, tied his legs together, and laid him on the veranda to sober up. Thus restrained, the chiefs of the river villages and all the important men of the upper Tatau River lay about on Chief Ladah's veranda like pigs trussed up for market.

Startled by a sudden burst of noise, Nyla raised her eyes from the row of fallen great men and ran to the far end of the veranda. There the powerful young Chief Sawa was fighting with one of the posts that held up the roof. He struck it with his hands, banged it with his head, and cursed it with all the profane words in the Dyak tongue. He filled the air with his shouts and curses, and the village police seemed powerless to do anything with him.

Whether he slipped on the dirty bamboo floor or threw himself forward with intentional violence Nyla couldn't tell, but he fell heavily and with a deep groan. His foot had broken through the split bamboo floor.

The village police pulled him back out of the hole, but Nyla could see that Sawa's hand was hurt. His hand seemed to be broken at the wrist. Bones stuck out through the flesh, and blood spurted from an ugly wound.

"What shall we do?" the frightened men inquired. "What shall we do?"

Chief Ladah lay helpless on the veranda floor. Malik snored beside one of the wine jars. Chief Sidang, blubbering and shouting, was just being tied down. There was no one to help, no one to answer.

One of the women brought some young banana leaves and bound them tightly around the wounded hand to stop the bleeding, and the young Chief Sawa was left to sober up as best he could.

Nyla, still dressed in her gorgeous feast jewelry, stood looking down upon the drunken chiefs and other important men of the river. They lay helpless in drunken stupor scattered about both inner and outer verandas of her father's longhouse.

She looked at Malik. He had been snoring in a heavy slumber since noon; and Chief Ladah, her father, was tied up like all the other men who had gotten too violent for the police to handle.

The girl turned away from the dismal sight. The feast was over. The stench of spilled wine, rotten fish, and other worse smells, polluted the air. Two broken wine jars spewed the dregs of their contents on the inner veranda floor.

Nyla hurried to the notched-log ladder that led down toward the riverbank above the wharf. Part way down the ladder, she turned back and went to her mother.

"Please, Mother, take these things off. I am so tired."

Mother unfastened the heavy brass ornaments and put them away in a box at the end of her sleeping mat. The two did not talk. They both knew what had happened, and what was there to say?

With a feeling of delicious lightness, Nyla hurried down to the river. But she was troubled. The great spirit feast was over, but it had brought no pleasure. Would her father be blamed for this accident? Chief Sawa was much loved by his village people. He was young and handsome, and his family idolized him; they were sure to be angry about his hurt arm. Who had ever seen a chief with a hand all broken like that? Could it be put straight again? How could Sawa ever carry a spear or row a boat? Who ever heard of a chief who couldn't throw a spear or paddle a dugout? When everyone sobered up, wouldn't they say that Chief Ladah was to blame? They would say he had not appointed enough police, or that his floor was rotten.

Nyla stood shivering on the riverbank. It was just bad luck, bad luck. The spirits were still angry, and the feast had done no good at all. She looked out over the swift river. It had risen. There must have been a heavy rain somewhere.

Then she saw the boat—the small white boat that belonged to the teacher, Poojee. Down it came with its one rower, rocking through the boiling current, skimming over the muddy water like a winged bird. Nyla remembered how Malik had driven the young teacher from their village only a few days ago. Would he come back? Would he dare to come to this village when the witch doctor had forbidden him?

The boat turned and came toward Ladah's wharf. It nosed in among the tossing dugouts already tied there, and Poojee fastened his boat and leaped out onto the wharf of floating logs.

Nyla did not run away as she had the first time Poojee came to their village. She stood watching the teacher fasten his boat, but she did not say anything. She looked into the teacher's face and saw that he smiled at her. Then he spoke to her in her own language.

"You are the chief's daughter, aren't you?"

Nyla nodded her head and a flash of shame burned through her as she recalled how Malik had dragged her in front of the teacher and screamed out the story of the Kayan girl's curse.

"Are you having a feast here today?" Poojee looked about at all the decorated dugouts tied to the wharf.

Nyla nodded again.

"Is your father home?"

"Yes," she said in a low voice.

"Take me to him," Poojee said. "My God has sent me a message that your father needs me."

Nyla felt as though a flash of lightning had struck at her. She understood the teacher's words well, but how could he know that her father needed help, that they all needed help, that a terrible accident had happened and no one knew what to do?

"Did the drums call you?" She could think of no other way such a message could travel to Sidang village where Poojee was living, yet she knew that no drum had been beaten. It would have been no use; all the river chiefs were gathered here.

Again a smile crossed the young man's face. "The drums of God," he said. "They beat in here." He put both hands to his head. "God's word can travel faster than the light. But come, take me to your father."

Once on the longhouse veranda, the teacher looked down on the unconscious forms of Chief Ladah and all the other chiefs and principal men of Tatau River. Nyla saw surprise and pity in his eyes. Then he looked down at Nyla standing beside him.

"Is your mother here?" he asked.

Without speaking, Nyla led him to the door of their room

in the longhouse and called mother. She came out shaking water from her hands and explained that she was just washing rice for the evening meal.

"Is there trouble here?" Poojee asked.

"Yes, there is trouble." Mother looked at him with wonder in her face. "How did you know?"

Poojee smiled at her. "I knew. I just knew. I felt impressed to come. Tell me what's wrong."

Mother led him to the place where young Chief Sawa lay tied down to the floor.

With an expression of surprise and pity, Poojee knelt beside him. He tore away the banana-leaf dressing and took from his pocket a square of clean white cloth. He bound this around the arm. Blood welled up again from the torn wrist.

"Bring me a little stick," he said to Nyla.

She hurried away and came back with a small piece of bamboo.

"That's good." He put the stick inside the knot and twisted it until the flow of blood stopped again. Then he examined the wrist. With tender care he began to straighten it and make it lie along Sawa's side like the other one.

With wonder and terror Nyla watched the teacher bind up Chief Sawa's broken wrist—wonder because of the teacher's skill, and terror because he had been called by the "drums of God."

6

WITH wonder and terror in her heart, Nyla stood and watched the teacher bind up Chief Sawa's broken wrist—wonder because of the careful and skillful way he took care of the wound, terror because this teacher, Poojee, had come to their village, called by the "drums of God." Every time she thought about the unseen God who could call people like that, who knew all about everyone, shivers of fright ran up and down her spine. How great such a God must be!

Poojee spoke to mother. "You stay here and watch him. Don't let him move. Hold his hand like this till I get back."

Poojee ran down the notched-log ladder to the river and came back in a short time with a packet of strange things that he had brought from his boat. Nyla saw a roll of white stuff, soft as kapok, bottles, jars, and tins, which Poojee explained were different kinds of medicine.

Neither Nyla nor her mother, nor any of the village people who had gathered round, had ever seen anything like this medicine. It all looked so clean. Poojee unfolded another square of white cloth and laid the medicine on it. When he had finished with Sawa's hand, it was rigid with fresh strips of bamboo enclosing a pad, and a bandage of clean white material. Then, slowly he untied the first cloth he had wound around the wounded arm. After he had put all his medicine back into the packet, Poojee sat by Sawa's side for a long time without saying anything.

The village people went back to their work, all those who had not taken part in the feast. They began to clean up the village and to prepare food for their evening meal. Mother went to finish her cooking, but Nyla still sat with Poojee. Gradually relief filled her mind. She could see that Poojee had saved her father from great shame and trouble. Now, with such powerful medicine, Sawa's hand would surely be all right.

Still she kept thinking about how Poojee had come. "The drums of God," he had said. "The drums of God" had called him here. God knew about this feast. He could see all these drunken chiefs on the floor. He knew about Sawa. God must know about the crocodile, too, and about the Kayan girl's curse.

Nyla looked at Poojee and all at once a daring thought came into her mind. She wanted to ask him to sing again that song he had sung the first time he came to their longhouse, the song that began:

> "Within the mighty love of God,
> I am safe, always safe."

Of course she didn't say anything, but thinking of the song and what it meant made a light inside her, and Nyla felt herself glowing with joy and wonder and relief. She remembered something else Poojee had said, "God is greater than all the crocodiles and all the curses in the world."

Evening came on. The sun went down in a bank of black clouds, and still the teacher, Poojee, sat by the young chief, Sawa. He listened to Sawa's breathing and held the young chief's good hand and looked often at the wounded one; but the blood did not ooze through the bandage.

Hours went by, and Poojee seemed to relax. Nyla thought he slept a little sitting there on the bamboo floor. At last mother called her, and she went to her sleeping mat. All was well. God had come to Ladah's village. "I am safe, always safe."

Sometime during the night Nyla wakened. The beat of heavy rain on the roof disturbed her. Beneath the longhouse a dog howled. Wind whined under the high longhouse roof, and the surge of the tormented river rose and roared in her ears.

Now how will the chiefs get home? she asked herself. They may stay for days; and she thought of how much rice it would take to feed so many visitors. Then she remembered the teacher, Poojee. Was he still sitting out there on the veranda floor beside the wounded chief? She jumped up and ran to look.

The outer, open veranda was awash with sheets of rain driven by a stormy wind. Someone had dragged all the drunken visitors into the shelter of the inner veranda or into the rooms of the longhouse. Young Chief Sawa slept just inside the door of their own room. The teacher, Poojee, was gone.

Then Nyla realized that the day was breaking. The heavy storm made everything appear dark. She ran inside to find her mother making a fire in the clay stove on the floor at the end of their room.

"Oh, Mother, did the teacher go?"

"Yes, child, he went just a little while ago."

Nyla stood at the door of their room and looked out over the raging river. Flotsam and jetsam from its banks tossed and whirled in the muddy water. Fallen trees riding the crest of the current met and tangled with one another in eddies of the stream like giants in battle for mastery of the flood.

55

"How could he go, Mother? No one could go anywhere in the river as it is now."

"He went. He said there was a sick man in Sidang's village who needed him, and he wasn't afraid."

No, Nyla thought to herself, Poojee wasn't afraid of anything. He wasn't afraid of the crocodile, or of the Kayan girl's curse, or the storm, or the flooded river; and he had not been afraid to come back to Ladah's village when the "drums of God" called him, even though Malik had driven him away and told him never to return.

In spite of the clouded day, the heavy rain, and the roaring river, Nyla felt gladness bubbling inside her, and she knew why. The words of Poojee's song were coming true for her too.

"God is with me everywhere;
I am safe, always safe."

As the morning passed, some of the great men of the river villages sobered enough to look out over the swollen river and decided that they would spend the day resting. They chewed their quids of betel nut and ate the rice the women prepared.

Chief Ladah recovered enough to look languidly around, and the first object he saw was the very white bandage on young Chief Sawa's wrist.

"What's this?" he asked of the other men squatted under shelter of the inner veranda. "What happened? Who hurt Sawa?"

No one had an answer. The chief grabbed Malik and shook him. The witch doctor wakened in a surly mood. He sat up and looked about him, out at the storm, and then at the miserable-looking dignitaries who sat about chewing betel nut.

"Who shook me?" He scowled at all of them.

"I shook you," Chief Ladah said. "Look at that and tell us what it means." He pointed to the white bandage on young Chief Sawa's wrist.

Malik dragged himself to his feet and knelt by the still-sleeping Sawa. He lifted the bandaged hand, and Sawa jerked up with a howl of fury. He struck out with his good hand so violently that Malik fell back onto the veranda floor. Sawa looked down at his hand and wrist and began to moan and rock back and forth in great distress.

"Tell us what happened to you," Chief Ladah told the young man. "How did you get hurt?"

Sawa could tell them nothing. Not one of the chiefs or principal men of the villages could remember anything that had happened since yesterday. Finally Ladah called his wife and the men he had appointed as police. They had been resting too, for the duties of handling such a group of drunken great men had been difficult and tiring.

"Tell us, what does this mean?"

Then they told the chief how Sawa had gotten out of hand and hurt himself badly. They pointed out the broken floor beside the big post that held up the roof. They described the severe wound and showed the chief the bloodstains where the wrist had bled.

"Which one of you wrapped up his hurt wrist and straightened it with the bamboo like this?" Ladah asked.

Then his wife spoke up. "It was Poojee, the teacher who was here the other day—the one Malik sent away." She threw a sharp glance at the witch doctor. "He came just after Sawa was hurt. The drums of his God called him, and he knew that someone was hurt in this village."

Nyla saw the witchman's face come alive with anger. Malik was fully awake now; rage shook his voice. "How dare that teacher come back here and make his magic in this village!"

Again Malik went over to where Sawa sat moaning and tried to grab hold of his hurt arm. Sawa screamed and fought with such vicious strength that Malik could do nothing. Then the witch doctor tried to persuade him with words.

"This is dangerous magic," Malik told the young chief. "You will be cursed by every evil spirit on this river if you allow that white stuff to remain on your arm. Let me take it off."

"No, no, no!" Sawa shouted and got to his feet slashing out again at Malik until the witch doctor went into his own room in the longhouse and slammed the door.

The day began to fade early, for rain still fell, and now the river roared and raged out of its banks and over all the low bars and up the draws along the Tatau. The surface of the stream heaved and tumbled with the glut of water; great trees whirled past, and pieces of buildings, along with a battered dugout torn from its moorings at some upriver village wharf.

No one wanted to go home that night. No one would expect them to venture out in such weather. Even Sawa, who lived almost straight across the river, looked out at the tumult and shook his head, unwilling to venture out They all slept in Ladah's village that night.

Nyla wondered whether the white crocodile had come back to their creek, but when she went to look, the rain beat down with such fury that she could not see anything clearly except the swollen waters and the curtain of rain.

When Nyla's mother called her in to go to bed, the girl asked her, "What do you think Malik will do now? He was very angry."

"Yes, he hates that teacher and I can't see why, because if he had not come, Sawa might have bled to death, and then where would we have been?"

By morning the rain had stopped. Bright sunshine beat down on the still-swollen river as it raged past the villages tearing loose everything along its banks within reach of its sucking strength. Still the day was clear and pleasant, and one by one the chiefs and warriors left. They kept in close to the banks taking advantage of every cross current, and picked their way carefully. The people in Ladah's longhouse stood on their high veranda and watched them go, not sorry at all, because the rice bins of the village had suffered much the last day or two.

Last of all, Chief Sawa went. Since he could not creep along close to the banks but must cross over the wide river to his longhouse, he waited until the water had begun to go down. Some of the principal men from his village rowed his boat. He still held his hand carefully. He would not touch it himself, and he would not allow anyone else to touch it. He had not spoken any good words to Ladah. He listened to all the talk that buzzed about him, but said nothing. He kept looking at his injured hand and wrist as though he could not believe that the bandaged, splinted, aching thing could possibly belong to him.

The men of Ladah's village and some of the women stood on the log wharf watching Sawa and his men leave. Nyla could feel the uneasiness that spread through the company. She looked out into the troubled river. Swift dusk darkened the already clouded sky, for another storm was rising. Out in the rolling water, Nyla saw something—the gigantic form of the spirit crocodile, the creature they had all hoped was gone forever. She came on, now, in full sight of them all. She swished into the flooded creek and lay as though content to be at home once more.

A great sigh went up from all the villagers gathered on Ladah's wharf.

"You see." Malik spoke in a loud and angry voice. "You see, all our feasts and all our offerings and all our magic comes to nothing because that teacher brings his witchcraft here."

They dragged themselves up the notched log into the longhouse in discouraged silence. And the rain began again.

It was not till evening of the next day that the rain finally stopped and the sun shone on the mighty river, now in full flood. Several of the village people came down to the wharf to make sure that their boats were securely tied. Nyla stood at the veranda railing just above them, and she saw the log as soon as they did.

It was an enormous fallen tree with its branching roots riding high in the water. The log was caught in an eddy that formed a giant whirlpool right in front of Ladah's wharf. Even in slack water the eddy was there, but in flood time it swirled and sucked with vicious strength.

All the logs in Ladah's floating wharf had been caught in that *oolock,* as the Dyaks called the whirlpool, and swept in close enough so the men could rope them and de them up to shore. A battle with a big log in the flooded river needed the best brains and all the strength of the whole population. If the log was allowed to continue its whirling motion, it might come in closer and closer until it could tear the wharf loose from its moorings.

On the other hand, if the huge log could be captured and brought under control, it would make a noble addition to the wharf. There was good reason for all Ladah's men to rush to their boats and grapple with the floating prize.

Men raced up and down the notched-log ladder, bringing paddles from the inner rooms. They scurried into their boats while the women came down to the wharf with poles in their hands. When the circling log whirled in dangerously close to the wharf, they pressed against it with all their poles and eased it out into its circular track again. Nyla came down with her own pole, glad to do her part with the older women to protect the wharf until the men could bring the giant log under control.

Excitement grew. The log, contrary beyond reason, defied all efforts to draw it to the shore and lasso it. Each time Ladah's men seemed to have gentled the wayward tree, it broke away from them and continued its majestic journey round and round. At last it appeared to be circling farther out in the stream. In a few minutes it would be too far out to get a rope onto it.

At that moment Ladah called to Nyla, "Come, child. I need you."

He drew his dugout back against the wharf for an instant while Nyla sprang in beside him. With a few swift strokes of his paddle, he reached the log. Laying the canoe alongside, he told Nyla to jump onto the trunk of the fallen tree and make fast a stout line to the scraggled root.

Nyla did as she was told, but as she jumped onto the log, its balance, which was delicately poised, was upset and the enormous trunk turned over in a flash. Nyla clutched at the nearest of the roots and disappeared under the water.

When Nyla jumped onto the log its balance was upset, and the enormous trunk turned over in a flash. Nyla clutched at the nearest roots and disappeared under the water.

7

WHEN the log turned over and Nyla disappeared beneath the water, Chief Ladah waited in perfect confidence. Neither flood nor swift water was a perplexity to any Dyak in the water. Floods and swift water might be dangerous to boats, but never to a person, with the wharf so near and the water full of dugouts.

Every instant the chief expected to see his daughter come to the river's surface. He drew away from the log and looked about, continually widening the circle of his gaze, for he was being carried downstream at a rapid pace.

Then he turned his back on the tree, abandoned his dugout, and plunged into the river. The great log swung into the savage current and disappeared around the curve below Ladah's longhouse.

After an interval of anguished minutes, Ladah raised a mighty cry. He swam here and there in frantic despair, but all his search was fruitless. Night was closing in now, and there was no moon. All the strong men of the village threw themselves into the water, while the women wailed on the log wharf. Nyla's mother leaped into her own dugout, and with wild screams she paddled here and there in the gathering darkness, calling her daughter's name.

All was in vain. Everyone came back to the wharf. Someone had even caught the chief's boat and brought it back, but no one had found Nyla.

Early darkness settled over the wharf. The women climbed up the notched-log ladder into the longhouse, and the men followed. Chief Ladah was the last to go up. For a long time he stood on the rocking wharf, watching the flooded stream swirl past.

It seemed impossible that Nyla could have been taken by the flood. Surely the white crocodile must have been out there watching and waiting. The crocodile had taken her. The more Ladah thought about it, the more sure he became. The spirit of the Kayan girl had taken revenge in the crudest possible way.

With a groaning misery deep inside him, Chief Ladah climbed the ladder into the village. All his people had gathered on the open veranda. The women brought oil lamps and set them on the floor. The men sat in the usual council circle where they always met to discuss all events, good and bad. While the women wept softly in the background, the men sat and talked.

"You see," Malik said, "it is just as I told you. The spirit of the Kayan girl has come back, and it is she who has devoured the chief's daughter."

One of the village men spoke up. "It isn't possible that she could have drowned. She could swim as well as any fish, and her father was right there."

Another man said, "This may be our punishment for allowing that teacher, Poojee, to come and make his witchcraft in our village. We must not forget that."

The chief groaned. "The teacher, Poojee, came on the day of the feast, you remember. It was he who made medicine for Sawa's wound. He saved us from great shame and perhaps from much trouble."

Malik's small eyes flashed. He looked at the chief. "I suppose you want that teacher to come back now and tell us what we should do to get your daughter back from the crocodile."

Chief Ladah stared at Malik. "Yes, that is exactly what I am thinking. Tomorrow morning two of you men take a boat and go up the river to Sidang's village and bring Poojee back with you. He can't bring my child back from the crocodile's mouth, but maybe he can tell us what to do with the crocodile."

Ladah listened to the heartbroken wailing that came from his room in the longhouse and felt his own heart breaking with grief.

No one slept that night in Ladah's village. The noise of the drums and gongs deafened everyone, and between their beats, the sound of wailing lifted into the damp, warm air.

One woman ran from one end of the village to the other like a mad thing. Her long hair streamed behind her, and with every bound she uttered a wail that was all out of proportion to her size and age. She was Malik's old mother, leader of mourning, princess of weeping. On every occasion of grief among the river villages, people sent for her, because nature had gifted her with the ability to howl and shriek like no other creature on the river. No funeral procession ever paddled up the river without her. She always sat in the dugout that led the procession, and the banks of the river echoed with her terrifying cries.

Now with a frenzy of fury and grief, she shrieked to the river, the mountains, and the heavens, that Nyla, the chief's daughter, was gone—taken by the spirits of the river.

Chief Ladah could not rest, neither could he comfort his wife. She tore her long hair and rocked back and forth in an abandon of wild and desperate sorrow. A feeble oil lamp gave a dim light in the inner room of the longhouse. He looked at the empty mat where his daughter, Nyla, had slept all the years of her life. Now it was empty. Outside, the river rushed and raged through the darkness.

He thought about the great spirit feast and remembered how beautiful Nyla had looked, dressed in all her mother's jewelry, serving wine to the chiefs. He thought about all the time and hard work and the supply of rice they had used for the feast, and it was not enough. The spirits were still angry. Never in his life had Chief Ladah felt so helpless.

Yes, he must send for Poojee. He must see that those two men got away early tomorrow morning to go and get Poojee. Malik would object, but Ladah was the chief. The power was his. He would see to it that the teacher was called.

Just before dawn the wailing died down and the drums ceased their throbbing. The chief slept for a few minutes. But with the first sunrays he was up again and down at the water's edge. There had been light drizzling rain during the night, but the river was receding to its normal channels. Great logs no longer fought for room on its bosom, and the water was not quite so muddy. No one else was up. The grief and sorrow and violent weeping had left everyone exhausted.

As Chief Ladah stood gazing at the empty river, a new thought came into his mind. He himself would go and bring that teacher, Poojee. Why not? After all, who had a better right?

Without waiting longer and without saying a word to anyone, he untied his dugout, and laying a strong stroke to the paddle, he started upstream. Rowing against the swift current was a good thing for Ladah. He soon realized that keeping at work was absolutely necessary if he was to control his grief and handle his village affairs.

So, as morning crept over the mountain, he paddled madly toward Sidang's village. When he reached the log wharf below the longhouse where Poojee was staying, he saw that the village was already astir and ready to begin the day's work. But wait, what was that? The usual sound of crowing roosters, barking dogs, and squabbling children was hushed. Instead there came to his ears the sound of singing. Singing? Yes, the sound of singing.

Without waiting he tied his canoe to the log wharf and hurried up the notched-log ladder until his head was above the floor level and he could look into the inner veranda of the longhouse.

There, under the shelter of the roof's wide overhang, the whole village was gathered, and they were all singing a beautiful song. Poojee stood before them waving his arms and leading the singing with a clear, sweet voice and a big smile. Everyone who sat on the floor about him looked happy.

Chief Ladah stood for a moment, looking and listening, then he came up into the veranda. Poojee turned and saw him. The singing stopped at once. The teacher came to meet him. "Come in, come in. We know what brings you here. We have heard your drums, and we are ready to start for your village."

Then Chief Ladah sat down in the circle and told how his daughter had been taken by a spirit crocodile, the white crocodile in which the vengeful spirit of the Kayan girl lived and waited to punish the people of the village where she had been mistreated.

The people of Sidang village sympathized with Ladah, for they had lost relatives to crocodiles too, during past years. They knew how he suffered. The women wailed, and the men gathered around him with pitying words. Poojee had gone to his room, and now he came out with his paddle and a little bundle of belongings.

"I'm ready," he said. "Let's go."

"Shall I take my boat?" he asked Ladah at the wharf.

"No, get into mine. I want to talk to you, and I shall want you to stay a few days with us. We can bring you back."

In the boat going down the river both Poojee and the chief pulled hard on their paddles, and the dugout shot over the water with amazing speed.

Neither of them said much; they were too busy handling the little dugout in the swift river. It was not until they were making the boat fast to Ladah's wharf that Poojee asked, "What does Malik think about Nyla's disappearance?"

"Oh, he thinks it is the white crocodile. All of us do. Malik thinks that crocodile was after Nyla from the first time she came into our creek."

"Does the crocodile still come?" Poojee asked.

"No, that's a strange thing too. She used to come every night. But since we planned the feast we have not seen her so often."

"That's a strange circumstance," Poojee agreed. "Do you have any idea where the white crocodile has her den?"

"The Great White One would not have a den. Ordinary river crocodiles have the openings to their dens under water. Maybe their dens are caves deep under the riverbanks. Who knows? Malik says that the spirit crocodile wouldn't have a den. How could she?"

"Well." Poojee scratched his head. "If the big white crocodile did take the girl, she must have taken her somewhere. Which way did the crocodile come from when she came to your creek? You must have seen."

"She always came from downriver, and she always went downriver when she left our creek, but who knows what customs a spirit crocodile follows? She may have been trying to deceive us."

A boatload of warriors from Sidang had followed the two men down the river, and now they tied up at the wharf. They went up together into the longhouse veranda where Ladah's people were gathered, all talking excitedly. When the chief and Poojee came up, Malik cut off a loud and fierce speech he was making and turned an angry look on the teacher. He sat down now and refused to say anything more, as though brooding over some great wrong.

"We are making plans to kill the white crocodile," one of the village men explained.

Then Chief Ladah spoke to them. "You all know that the crocodile always brings its victim out after three or four days and pounds the body on a hard sand bar. After that the crocodile will eat the carcass." The chief shuddered and felt a ghastly sickness twist his stomach.

Even as they talked, shouts came from the river. Boats paddled in from upriver and down, filled with warriors who had heard the message of the drums and come to battle with the killer crocodile.

Chief Ladah's veranda was soon thronged with fierce, howling men eager for the hunt. It was of no use to remind them that the guilty crocodile could not be discovered for three or four days. Ladah could not restrain them. All this wild energy must be quickly directed, or fights and serious trouble would develop.

The chief roused himself from his grief. "All of you go. Scatter out and look for the white crocodile. You must not

Chief Ladah and Poojee sat alone on the quiet veranda. The sun was almost at midheaven.

"Tell me more about the magic of your God," Chief Ladah said.

attack her yet, but you may be able to see which way she goes. Then you will know which sandbanks to watch."

With howls of rage the warriors flung themselves down the notched-log ladder, leaped into their dugouts, and scattered in every direction, screaming, cursing, and paddling as though all the demons of Tatau River were after them.

Malik went into his room and shut the door. Chief Ladah and Poojee sat alone on the quiet veranda. The sun was almost at midheaven.

"Tell me more about the magic of your God," Chief Ladah said.

Poojee told him again the story of God's mighty power and His great love. Finally the chief asked him to sing the song that ended:

> "God is with me everywhere;
> I am safe, always safe."

"My daughter liked that song," the chief said. "I heard her singing it several times after you were here that first time. What does it mean?"

"It means that God is always with us, and we never need to be afraid."

"Do you call it safe when a crocodile takes a little girl?" The teacher looked kindly at the chief. "The life we have here and now must end sometime. Is that not true?"

"It is true," the chief admitted.

"We have another life—a life in God, which nothing can ever touch. That life is the important one. All who love God and believe in Him will have a life that never ends. Whatever happens to us, God permits it to come. Our lives are safe in His hands."

"Come." The chief got to his feet. "Come, I want you to explain to Nyla's mother all that you have told me." He led Poojee into his inner room in the longhouse.

So the day passed, in both weeping and comforting, and when the cool breeze wafted in soothingly, Chief Ladah laid his hand on the teacher's shoulder and said, "My heart is comforted. The magic of your God is good."

That evening all the warriors came back to Ladah's village. They had seen many crocodiles basking on riverbanks, sunning themselves with their mouths wide open, and crocodile birds flitting in and out of their cavernous jaws. Yes, they had seen dozens of crocodiles, but not the white crocodile.

The men were tired and willing to sit and listen to Poojee's words. "People of Ladah's village, and all you men from the river longhouses, I bring you a message from the God who made all things. He made crocodiles, too, and He can make them do what He wishes. He can prevent them from doing what He does not want them to do."

Malik came out of his room and took his place in the circle. His fierce little eyes darted from the teacher to Chief Ladah and then around the circle, but he did not speak.

Poojee continued, "I think, just as you do, that the white crocodile has taken the chief's daughter. We must keep on hunting until we find that crocodile. A killer crocodile must be destroyed. If the crocodile has eaten the girl, we will know."

The chief knew that Poojee's words were true, because every time the Dyaks had killed a crocodile that had eaten a human being, they always found metal bracelets or rings or necklaces in the creature's stomach. Once they even found a length of heavy chain.

"Don't be afraid, my friends." Poojee talked on. "The God

who made us allows us to lose those we love, but He is able to fill our hearts with His comfort. If we believe in Him we shall have peace."

All the men in the circle sat quietly. The chief held his head in his hands. Through the quiet air a slight sound of splashing water caught the ears of every person on the veranda. Malik leaped to his feet and ran to the veranda railing.

"Look!" he pointed. "The white crocodile has come to our creek this evening, and there she goes right now—back into the river. While you have sat like fools and listened to this teacher's smooth talk, the crocodile has escaped."

Then everyone ran to look, and they all saw the giant form of the Great White One riding the bosom of the river, floating downstream past the village.

8

WHEN the floating log had turned over, Nyla threw out both hands and grasped at the branching roots. In an instant, she realized that she must free herself from the roots in order to get her head above water. But her hair had loosened in the swift current, and the tangling of her long loose hair among the roots made the struggle so difficult that for a few desperate seconds she almost panicked.

She fought with the mass of roots. She pulled this way and that. She tore at her coarse hair. She braced herself against the rough trunk. Exerting every muscle in her body and all her shrewd wisdom of the water, she managed at last to tear herself free and get her head above the surface. She gasped in lungfuls of air while she still clung to the log. Recovered a little, she clutched at the upper side of the floating tree.

Night was coming down fast, and Nyla saw that she had already been swept around the curve below her village. Not a dugout was in sight. The noise of the rushing river surged in her ears, but there was no human voice or sound. She knew that she must cling to the log, or be swept away in the flooded stream. She struggled up till she lay across the upper side of the plunging log, and there she rested for a little while.

The log was still close to the bank, but it was hurrying along in the swift current with such force that any effort to control it was useless. Nyla thought of diving into the water and swimming ashore. She was an excellent swimmer and not afraid of water, but darkness had settled over the river, and she could not see whether the bank of the stream presented a wall of rock or a mass of soft ferns. Neither one would be possible to climb. She dared not leave the log without knowing that she could climb out of the water at the river's edge.

The log shot forward into the darkness.

On the banks of Tatau River there grows a branching tree that blossoms during the flood season. Its flowers are small, insignificant dots, and one can scarcely see them at all from a few feet away; but these tiny blooms attract the fireflies that abound in that region. When darkness comes down on the jungle such trees sparkle with millions of tiny twinkling lights.

Nyla knew about these fire-spirit trees. She had often seen them while passing up or down the river in her father's dugout. Like all the river Dyaks, she had a terrible fear of a tree that attracted such countless little fire-spirits.

The floating log with its lone passenger had now been carried past three bends of the river. Nyla raised her eyes and saw one of the fire-spirit trees hanging over the bank. The dancing lights threw a faint glow into the darkness. She calculated the distance and direction of her floating log and knew it would pass directly under the fire-spirit tree. Her heart pounded in wild terror. Dare she touch the spirit tree? She had only an instant to decide.

The huge floating tree plunged under the spangled branches, the high-riding root tore away twigs and small limbs, then it raced on down the river; but Nyla no longer clung to its broad trunk.

Grasping the thin branches that dipped into the flooded stream, she drew herself up monkey-wise into a crotch of the tree. A great disturbance arose among the tiny fire-spirits, but Nyla paid no attention to them. "I am safe, safe!" She spoke the words aloud, and instantly the words of Poojee's song rang in the night as though shouted in her ears:

> "God is with me everywhere;
> I am safe, always safe."

She rested then in the crotch of the branching tree above the roaring river.

As she rested, her mind went back to the feast She thought of Sawa's wounded hand and the unexpected coming of the teacher, Poojee. The "drums of God" had called Poojee, he had told them. A new thought struck the girl. God must be everywhere and know all about everything. No one could get away from Him.

The rain began again, a light drizzle. It was not cold, but it was not comfortable either. Through the long wet night Nyla twisted and turned, trying to find some position where she could rest. The gray morning found her still wedged in the crotch of the fire-spirit tree. Then the rain stopped, and the sun came out bright and beautiful over the rain-washed jungle and the furious river.

Now surely someone would come and find her. She looked about and decided that she knew this spot Not far back from the riverbank was a small plateau high enough so the floodwaters had not reached it. She recognized it as the forsaken clearing where Malik, the witch doctor, had planted his rice last season. He had raised a fine crop. Then, just before harvest, he had been crossed by dreadful omens, twice in a single day. An evil bird had called and fluttered down his path to the field, and a spotted snake had wriggled along on the ground in front of him. No Dyak would disregard such warnings. Malik had never been back. Nyla was sure of that.

She also remembered that Malik had laid a curse on this particular spot in order to warn all the river people away. Perhaps the sticks and stones that made a sign of the taboo were still here.

Nyla moved her stiff legs and tried to plan what she must do next. It was no use to stay in the tree. The discouraging thought pressed into her mind that since Malik had laid his curse on this sandbank, no boat was likely to come along this side of the river. They would all swing over to the opposite side of the stream, and no one could see the fire-spirit tree from so far away.

A more comforting idea also occurred to her. She knew that wherever a Dyak makes a rice field he also makes a shelter of bamboo and palm leaves where he may rest during the heat of the day and may even sleep at night to watch over the growing crop. Malik must have made such a shack here. She stretched and peered through the branches, but she could see no sign of a hut, only a couple of big sago palms waving thick wet fronds in the wind. Even though she couldn't see it, she knew that there must be a shack of some kind back there. She decided to get down from the tree and look around.

The river, still in flood, roared wild and swift below her. The trunk of the tree leaned far out over the water, and because of the flood, the tree stood in the water. She could not tell how deep or swift the water might be on the landward side of the tree, but she must risk crossing it. Fastening her hair in a tight knot, she climbed along the sloping trunk, leaped into the water, and swam without difficulty to dry land.

Now she stood at the edge of the abandoned rice field. It was, as she had guessed, Malik's last year's garden. The heavy growth of rice had matted down into a soggy mass of brown stalks. Here and there she saw the sprouting of *padi* that had never been harvested.

Then she saw the hut, or *lankau,* as she called it, at the back of the clearing under the shade of the sago palms. "Now I am safe. I even have a house." She spoke to herself. "If it is broken and spoiled, I know how to repair it."

With good courage and a much lighter heart, she approached the hut It stood on eight sturdy poles. The walls of split bamboo were not much damaged, but the roof was blown in and ruined. Nyla quickly calculated how many sago leaves it would take to make a new roof. With the sago trees so near, roofing such a small hut would be no problem at all. Nyla had often helped her mother make sago-leaf thatch, and she knew how to tie the leaves to the roof with thin strips of rattan.

"Now all I need is a knife," she said to herself. "Since Malik was frightened away so suddenly, possibly he might have left one here."

She looked all about the hut, lifted the fallen thatch, and scuffed her bare feet through the rubbish under the hut. Finally she went up the little bamboo ladder and stood on the floor of the hut And then she saw a knife. It was rusty, and the point was broken off, but it was a knife. All Malik's knives were good. He forged them himself. The knife was stuck between the bamboo wall and one of the posts.

Standing there with Malik's knife in her hand, an intense longing for home rushed over her. What would her father and mother be doing now? What would they think had happened to her? Wouldn't they try to find her? Surely they would come any minute. How could she let them know where she was? "Oh, if I only had a drum," she cried out.

Three miles of uncut virgin jungle lay between Nyla and her father's village. No Dyak had ever cut a path so far. They cut only short paths back to gardens on the riverbank. The river was the only highway.

"When the water goes down, I'll get out on that sandbank. Then someone might possibly see me. It's my only chance."

Nyla fondled the knife. She mused over its value. With the knife she could live for several days alone in the clearing. She plunged it into the ground again and again to clean off some of the rust. The knife was curved and as long as a man's forearm, graceful and well balanced and sharp even yet. Malik must have discarded it because the point was broken.

Under the hut Nyla found a smooth stone upon which such a knife could be sharpened. She worked over it with hopeful energy, smoothing, sharpening, and shaping the broken point to a new rounder one, but still keen.

As the sharp noise of the knife against the stone rasped in her ears, she began again to feel her desperate loneliness. She was all alone, one small girl against all the evil spirits that had cursed this spot and driven Malik away.

She sprang to her feet and looked about in defiance. "If the good spirits favor me," she screamed into the empty forest, "I will ask my father, the great chief of Ladah village, to make rich offerings."

She sat down beside the sharpening stone, struck with weakness and a feeling that she had done something wrong. Again the words of Poojee's song came back to her:

"God is with me everywhere;
I am safe, always safe."

The jungle was not empty. God was here. God was everywhere, and God must be greater than all the spirits. Hadn't Poojee told them that God had made everything? It was not the spirits, but God she should speak to. With the sharpened knife in her hands, she lifted her eyes to the sun-filled heaven and cried out, "O God, You who are everywhere, I believe You. I need You. Show me how to thank You."

Nyla felt in that moment a curtain of protection drop between her and the dangers of the jungle. Courage flowed into her, and as she cut leaves from the sago palm, she sang Poojee's song.

Now the jungle bird songs, the chattering monkeys, and the hum of insects in the forest sounded friendly. Nyla found the fiber she needed for sewing the thatch. She bent the green sago leaves and stitched them together so the hard rib of the leaf was at the top, and the thick doubled leaves made a long fringe below. There was no rattan, so she found some long, tough roots that would do, and she used them to tie the green thatch to the roof. Her deft fingers had finished half of the tiny hut when she saw that the sun was sinking. Then she realized that she was hungry.

Now she sat on the little ladder of the hut and wondered what she would eat. She knew that sago was nourishing food, but she loathed it. There would be time enough to eat sago when all other possibilities had been tried. A clump of bananas grew behind the hut, but the fruit was green. Only one object offered her any hope of acceptable food, and that was the decaying stump of a pinang palm, but the sun was going down now and she was too tired to do anything more.

She found an old roll of mats in the hut. The outer ones were damp and moldy, but the one in the center could be used. She spread it out under the thatched half of the roof and lay down to rest. The adventure of the night before had tired her. She was not accustomed to sleeping with a blanket, and the mosquitoes did not bother her. She slept.

Nyla woke early, and her first thought was thankfulness because no rain had fallen during the night. Then she lay on her mat, thinking for a long time of her father. What was he doing today? Would he come to find her? Then she sat upright, jerked into sudden fear by a thought so true that she must accept it. *They would think that the white crocodile had taken her.* And they wouldn't look for her. No, of course not. They would look for the white crocodile.

Even this discouraging thought could not keep Nyla's mind off her stomach. She was hungry. She had not eaten since the day before yesterday. Looking down from her *lankau*, Nyla saw the glint of water between the trees in the opposite direction from the river, and she pushed her way through the brush until she stood on the bank of a little stream. She followed its curving bed until she could see where it joined the river at a sharp angle. She tried to think of the creek's name. Then she remembered, Batoo Creek. It was called so because of the many big stones at the mouth of the stream. *Batoo* means "stone."

Not ten yards from the mouth of the stream, Nyla found a flat rock that made a fine washing platform. She dipped in the gurgling water and scrubbed herself with a round, rough stone. She washed her short, handwoven skirt, thumping and rubbing it on the flat rock. Then she put on the wet skirt and

Just coming out from the roots of a big tree, at the sharp angle where the creek joined the river, was the white crocodile. Nyla waited breathless as the crocodile pushed into the river.

parted the overhanging branches to look out on the river.

Just coming out from the roots of a big tree, at the sharp angle where the creek joined the river, was the white crocodile! Nyla might have been part of the stone she stood upon. She did not move an eyelash or loosen her hold on the branches. She waited, breathless, until the crocodile pushed out into the main stream of the river and disappeared. So, the Great White One lived here, on this creek! She must have her den under the bank!

As Nyla went back to her hut, she wondered—Was it really true that the Kayan girl's spirit lived in that crocodile? One thing was clear. No one had caught the white crocodile yet, although there must be people from her father's village looking for her.

Nyla picked up her knife and began hacking at the decayed stump of the pinang palm. It was a good-sized stump. Malik must have cut the palm down during last year's planting season. The stump was thoroughly rotted. She soon had it laid on the ground before her, and with one blow she split the whole six-foot length wide open. With a cry of delight, she knelt beside one of the halves and began exploring the decayed brown pulp with her fingers.

In an instant she drew out an enormous yellow grub as long as a man's index finger and very fat for its length. She swallowed several times and then, with great self-control, she laid the grub on a piece of banana leaf. In spite of her great hunger, Nyla was a dainty person and would not snatch at her food even though she was starving.

She finally clawed out the last hit of rotten pith in one half of the palm stump. A dozen of the huge yellow grubs lay on the banana leaf. She covered the other half of the stump and weighted the protecting banana leaves down with stones.

Now she sat on the top rung of the ladder leading up into her hut. In her hand she held the delicious breakfast she had dug from the palm stump. One by one, she ate the grubs. Then she went to Batoo Creek for a cold drink.

9

WHILE Nyla was trying to look after herself in Malik's old garden, wondering all the time when someone would come to rescue her, many things were happening at home.

Poojee was in Ladah's village, and for two days all the men from that village, as well as many warriors from other longhouses on the Tatau, wearied themselves with frantic rowing up and down the river. Chief Ladah commanded them to keep every sandbank on both sides of the river under constant observation, but Poojee suspected that the men spent more time in wild screaming, flourishing of spears, and threatening gestures than in actual patient guarding of the sand bars, which they must do in order to capture the wary crocodile.

Tormenting thoughts troubled the young teacher's mind. He could see that all the river people regarded the white crocodile with superstitious fear. They made a great pretense of hunting for the creature, but Poojee doubted that any of them would have the courage to attack her if they found her, because they thought she was a spirit crocodile.

Poojee felt sure Nyla had been taken by a crocodile—the river swarmed with all sizes of crocodiles. He knew she could not have drowned. No Dyak ever drowned unless held forcibly under the water.

It was now noon of the third day after Nyla's disappearance.

Neither the chief nor Poojee had gone out hunting with the village men. Although this day and tomorrow were the days on which the men were sure to find the guilty crocodile, still Ladah did not choose to go.

"I cannot bear to see my daughter in the crocodile's mouth," Ladah said. "And I don't want to see her dragged out onto some sandbank."

Poojee knew there was another reason, too. With all the village men gone, the place was quiet, and there was time for more talk about God and His power and His great love. The chief, with a childlike faith, had accepted the "new magic," and Poojee could see that both Ladah and his wife were comforted.

The sun was at midheaven, and the two men leaned against the railing of the outer veranda where the women pounded rice, wove mats and baskets, and tended their babies.

"Look!" The chief pointed a trembling finger toward the water. The white crocodile was swimming up the river only a few yards away from the wharf! Poojee marveled at the creature's size. Both he and the chief cried out in surprise, and all the women and children came to look.

As they watched, the crocodile lifted her head out of the water, then dived down and out of sight. The women began to weep in fright, and children clung to their mothers in terror.

"You see," Chief Ladah said. "There is war between the crocodile people and the Dyaks. Now what shall we do?"

Poojee had no answer. It was not an uncommon sight—a crocodile sticking its head out of the water, even close to the villages; but this crocodile was a strange pale color, and the biggest one the teacher had ever seen.

Nyla's mother began to weep. Hugging her little son,

86

Djeelee, close to her, she squatted on the bamboo floor and rocked back and forth in a frenzy of grief.

"You will see," Malik's mother said—she who was chief wailer for all the river villages. "You will see. That crocodile will come back tomorrow at this same time. She is begging for something."

"Oh, no, I don't think so," Poojee said. "How could that be? The crocodiles can't tell time."

"The crocodiles can see the sun," the old woman insisted. "And the crocodile people are angry with the Dyak people. You will see. That crocodile will come back tomorrow."

When the men returned from their hunt that evening, they admitted that they had looked everywhere and no one had seen the white crocodile or anything of the lost girl.

"But the Great White One was here today when the sun was at midheaven," Chief Ladah told them. "You remember she was here in our creek last night, too."

Then Malik, who had led the hunt that day, spoke. "She is a spirit crocodile and she is angry with this village. You will never take her on any sandbank. You will never kill her with a spear. She will come to this village again and again until Chief Ladah shuts his ears to the magic of this stranger."

The witch doctor stalked off to his room and closed the door.

Poojee looked at Chief Ladah.

"Go ahead, tell us stories or teach us songs," Ladah said. "The magic of your God has taken me, and I cannot turn back, no matter what Malik says."

Encouraged by the chief's words, the people settled down to listen while Poojee told them about other animals that God had made to obey Him.

He told of a man named Daniel who had been thrown into a den of lions. The Dyaks had never seen a lion, but they had seen jungle wildcats, and Poojee explained that lions were enormous cats that could easily kill people and often did; but God protected Daniel. He stayed all night with the lions, and they didn't harm him.

He told the story of Jonah and the great fish. The people could understand about a big fish because some rather large fish lived in the river, and some of them had big mouths. They could imagine a fish big enough to swallow a man. This man, Jonah, had run away from God; but he was God's man, and God sent the fish after him, and the fish swallowed him and brought him back.

He told them about how one of God's men was hungry and the ravens brought him food, not just once, but twice a day for quite a while. They understood about big black birds, for there were many such birds along the river.

He told them of how, when Jesus was here on this earth, He made a fish bring up a coin for a man who needed it and hadn't a coin in his pocket.

"So you see," Poojee concluded his stories, "if God can make a lion tame, if He can use a fish to bring back a man who has run away, if He can tell birds to feed a hungry man and show a fish where to get money, He can manage crocodiles, too. God has made them all."

Murmurings ran about the circle. The people enjoyed the stories, but they enjoyed the singing more, and Poojee taught them the same songs the Sidang people already knew. The warriors from Sidang's village sang out in clear, loud voices, proud to be able to join the teacher in making such fine music.

At last everyone went to sleep and the village grew quiet,

but Poojee was troubled and could not sleep. Although he had lived all his life in tropical countries where crocodiles are plentiful, yet he had been born and reared in a mountain village where no crocodiles ever came. He really didn't know much about crocodiles. He needed to know more—a lot more.

He knew that the stories he had told the people this evening had been for his own comfort, too. Certainly God must control all these creatures of the jungle rivers. Poor little Nyla. He hardly dared let himself think of her. After an hour of prayer the teacher unrolled his mat in the usual place on the inner veranda.

The following morning all the boats went out again to search the river. Even Ladah went, but Poojee stayed in the village. Malik would not consent to take him along. With real anxiety the teacher waited for the sun to reach the zenith.

Again he stood on the veranda along with every other human being who remained in Ladah's village. Yes, something moved in the water. Something rippled just under the surface. Then, beyond the log wharf, in almost the identical spot where she had risen yesterday, the white crocodile thrust her snout out of the water and the whole length of her pale body rested on the surface. Again she lifted her head, almost as though she had a word of advice for Ladah's village but could not utter it. Then she disappeared.

Poojee was speechless. He was glad Chief Ladah was gone. He would not have been able to face the chief's eager questions. What could it mean? He had never heard of such a thing before. He had been born into a Christian home and educated to be a Christian teacher. He did not believe in curses or omens. He did not believe that spirits of the dead come back to torment the living. Yet, why was this crocodile coming back to this village?

The teacher went to sit on his mat and think. Malik's mother had said yesterday that the crocodile would be back today. How could she know? Surely the Lord in heaven must have control of the creature. And why hadn't the warriors stayed in the village today when they knew that the crocodile was expected? He was sure, now, that none of them wanted to confront the spirit crocodile, as they called her.

All around him the village had sprung into activity. Women hurried about carrying water, preparing food, and a buzz of talk filled the air. The few old men who remained in the village began to build a raft. It was about four or five feet square and made of bamboo lengths, so it would float They lashed the bamboos together with rattan, and the whole raft was solid —a neat little floating platform.

Poojee soon found out what the women were doing. They were preparing cakes and goodies of all kinds. They intended to make an offering to the crocodile. The teacher was surprised at their certainty that the crocodile would come back again tomorrow.

And the crocodile did come back on the following day, at exactly the same time. She not only lifted her head, but turned herself in the river so that she faced the village and opened her enormous mouth as though giving forth some royal command. Then she sank away out of sight. The women hurriedly set the raft of food afloat, and the men, using their paddles, pushed it out into the river where it floated along with the current.

Poojee ran down to the wharf, untied one of the dugouts, jumped in, and paddled downstream. He could not understand what he had seen, but he was determined to find out more about the crocodile. Had she really been begging for food? If so, why? Did a crocodile have that much intelligence? Could she know that if she came back to the village repeatedly the people would offer her food? Would a crocodile relish such food? Poojee didn't know any of the answers, but he meant to find out all he could.

He had not paddled far before he realized that the great crocodile was swimming just under the water and not far ahead of him, but behind the little floating platform loaded with food. Poojee paddled quietly, keeping the raft under constant observation. It floated around the big curve below Ladah's village, then down, down, around two more bends of the stream. Then Poojee discovered what appeared to be the mouth of a small stream flowing into the main river at a sharp angle.

The crocodile was close to the raft now, perhaps even poking it a little with her nose. Poojee couldn't see. Anyhow the raft was going into the mouth of the small stream. No doubt the crocodile really did relish human food and had guided the raft into this quiet spot in order to enjoy it at leisure.

Poojee had seen enough. He looked all around in the water, but the crocodile had disappeared. The teacher turned back, glad that he had seen such a sight with his own eyes, otherwise he might not have believed it. He decided that crocodiles must have far more intelligence than people think.

Back at the village, he discovered that the hunting canoes had all come home with their usual report of failure. He questioned the chief and the older men carefully.

"Yes," they said. "Crocodiles often come to beg food; but they always come when the spirits are angry—when the crocodile people intend to eat some person."

"But this time a person is already taken," Poojee reminded them.

Poojee watched the raft drift to the mouth of a small stream. The crocodile was close to it now, perhaps even pushing it with her nose, for it moved into the mouth of the creek.

"How do we know? Perhaps others are going to be taken."

The chief rolled himself a quid of betel nut. "You see, the Great White One wanted food. Perhaps she will not come again."

Poojee puzzled long over the happenings of the day. Yet his faith began to rise. "Surely the Lord is in this place," he told himself. "All that has happened must be part of God's plan. There are men here from almost every village on the river, and now they have all heard about God. Would this have happened otherwise? Probably not." Yet, every time he thought of Nyla, he shuddered. The poor child, taken by the awful crocodile in the flood and the darkness! Why did such a terrible accident have to happen? He could not explain the crocodile's begging for food, but he accepted this, too, as part of God's plan.

That evening the white crocodile came back to the little creek below the village. Malik discovered her. He rushed up into the longhouse brandishing his knife, and shouted to everyone to come and help him kill the crocodile.

"No," Chief Ladah said. "Today we have made offerings of peace to the Great White One. Should we now go out to kill her? You have already told us that no spear can hurt this spirit crocodile. You know it is not our custom to destroy any crocodile unless we find a Dyak in its mouth or claws. I am not sure that this crocodile has taken my daughter. None of us can be sure until we find her body. Shall we anger the crocodile people and make more trouble?"

"You are a fool!" Malik screamed, and his face twisted with fury. "You are already a captive of this new magic. Drive this teacher from your longhouse before every evil spirit on the river comes to curse you."

Poojee did not wait to hear the chief's reply to Malik's outburst. He descended the ladder that led down from the end of the longhouse farthest from the river.

He stood on the bank of the little stream. Even in the starlight the pale form of the gigantic crocodile shone in the shallow water. Crocodiles, crocodiles, crocodiles and the gospel of God; what could they have to do with each other?

Something like admiration rose up in his mind toward the savage creature lying there in the creek. For a long time he stood close enough to reach out and touch her, yet she did not move. Poojee was sure now that this one was no bloodthirsty killer. Doomed to be a creature of dread and a symbol of wickedness, yet even this crocodile was certainly under the control of the God who had made her.

As the wind, the waves, and the fury of men were under God's direction, so were the crocodiles of Tatau River. Poojee could not understand all he had seen during these days in Ladah's village, but his faith burned bright again.

As he turned to leave the creek bank, the mighty crocodile turned too and slipped out into the river.

When Poojee climbed up to the longhouse veranda, he found it empty. Everyone had gone to bed. He lay down on his mat and slept.

10

NYLA spent her second morning at the clearing putting the rest of the thatch on her little hut. Often she looked toward the river. Her only hope must come from some passing boat. Yet she knew that ever since Malik saw the bad omens last year the Dyaks avoided this side of the stream.

Her skin was brown, her short handwoven skirt was brown too, and from a distance a small brown object would be difficult to see.

When she had tied the last length of sago thatch in place, she went toward the riverbank. The water had gone down, and the sandbank lay exposed just below the edge of the rice field. Then she saw the forked sacks and the stones that made the *taboo* sign of her tribe. In keenest fright she ran back. Not for her life would she step on that forbidden sand bar. No person was allowed to remove a *taboo* except the one who had placed it there, and Nyla knew that Malik always made his curses as long-lasting as possible. She went back to her *lankau,* the hut beside the rice field.

Flood time was the season for jungle fruit, and Nyla decided to look along the creek for fruit trees. She needed a basket, but there was no basket anywhere about the old hut. She finally went to the creek with nothing but her handwoven skirt for carrying.

She found plenty of fruit, but it was high in the trees. She climbed one tree and filled her skirt with the rich, dark-red *rambutan* fruit. Four times she made the trip to the fruit trees and back to the hut. Then, convinced that she had enough fruit for a few days, she sat down and ate her second meal in the lonely clearing.

The next morning when Nyla went to bathe, it occurred to her that if she could get out to the mouth of the creek some passing boat might see her. As she stood on the flat rock, faint sounds reached her ears—the hunting cries of her people.

By swimming and wading and slipping around the big stones, she finally reached the tree roots where she had seen the white crocodile disappear. Far out in the river she saw several dugouts rowing swiftly up the stream on the turning tide. No shouting of hers could reach them. The riders were making far too much noise themselves. They did not even look in her direction.

She went back to her clearing, dug the grubs out of the other half of the palm stump, and ate her breakfast. As the third night drew on, she eyed the sago with interest. "I shall have to eat it," she prodded herself, "but not tonight."

On the fifth morning after Nyla was cast away on the abandoned rice field in the curve of Batoo Creek, she rose early after a wakeful night. In spite of wild fruit and grubs, the chief's daughter was very hungry. She went down for her morning bath and looked to see whether the white crocodile was anywhere around. She had begun to look forward to seeing her.

This morning no crocodile appeared, and Nyla went back to her hut more lonely than she had been since she came to this place. "If I'm going to live here a long time, I may as well make some proper water bamboos," she said aloud.

She looked about for a likely clump of bamboo. She had

noticed a large thicket of giant bamboo near the river, but it was close to the forbidden sandbank. Now she began to wonder whether the bamboo would be *taboo* because the sand bar was. She thought about it for a long time and then decided that the clump of bamboo was not actually on the sand. Wading through waist-high *lalang* grass, she used her knife to cut a beautiful length of bamboo just the right size for making joints to carry water.

She dragged it to the hut, cut it into suitable lengths, then took it down to the creek and weighted it down with stones. The bamboo must soak under water for several days until the greenness was cured out of it, then it could be dried and used.

"I may as well cut another," she said as she sharpened her knife on the stone under the *lankau*. "I could even pound some of these bamboo lengths flat and build a little porch onto my house. They would make a good floor."

Again she waded through the *lalang* grass to the clump of bamboo. The shoots were of all ages. Some were old and yellow, others young and green. Several new sprouts crisscrossed one another in graceful confusion. An old log lay across the bamboo thicket, and the young shoots tangled over and around it. The log must have lain there for a long time.

Nyla stepped up onto the log, then slipped and fell with her arm across it. *The log was a living creature.* She did not scream. She made no hurried movement. So great was the horror that fell on her, that she seemed to herself to crawl back to her hut. Actually her feet flew over the rough ground, but she uttered no sound. Rather would she die of silence than waken that dreadful sleeper. She scrambled up into her hut and hid in the darkest corner.

At last her senses returned and she was able to think more

Nyla stepped up onto the log, then slipped and fell across it. The log was a living creature. It was a big snake that could kill a deer or a man with a single blow.

clearly about this new trouble. It was a big snake, one of the varieties that live in the swamps of the Dyak country. Nyla knew that such a snake could kill a deer or a man with one blow from its powerful head. Then he would crush his prey by coiling about it and squeezing it until all the bones were broken. Last of all, he would cover the carcass with slime and swallow it whole. If the animal was large, the swallowing might take a long time, but the big snake never needed to hurry. After a meal the snake would sleep for a full moon of days, sometimes longer.

Then, when he awakened, he would be driven with great hunger, and he would hunt out the nearest animal that offered hope of a satisfying meal.

"Oh, my Father," Nyla moaned with anxiety. "Oh, Father, I shall die in the mouth of the great snake!"

Then, like a light, the words of Poojee's song came back to her. "God made the snake," she said in wonder. "Yes, God made the snake, and God is here. I am safe. I am safe."

Nyla knew a great deal about the jungle creatures. She knew that after a python eats a full meal there is a bulge in its stomach. The bulge stays there for a long time—until the animal he has swallowed is fully digested. Only after the bulge is gone does the snake waken and hunt for food. She knew what she had to do. She must go back and look at the snake again and see whether he had any bulge in him.

Holding to her new faith in the God who is everywhere, she picked her way back to the bamboo. This time she took a long look at the python. He had been there a long time, that was certain. New bamboo shoots had grown up, over, and around him. Some of them were fifty feet long and unbelievably strong. Yes, there was still a fat place in the snake's smooth

99

length, not large, but enough to reassure her. The snake would not waken for a few days, two or three at least. The only way to be sure was to come back every morning and look.

As she ran back to her *lankau,* Nyla found her courage returning. The snake would not waken this day. Perhaps she could think of some way to get home. "If I could only stay out at the mouth of the creek all the time, someone would surely see me," she said to herself.

She went down to the creek and waded to the mouth. The tide was low and the river current very swift. The creek was lower than she had yet seen it. She stood now beside the roots where she was sure the white crocodile had her den. Hanging to the roots with great care and planting her feet firmly on the rocks of the stream, she braced herself and gazed out into the angled rocky entrance where the creek joined Tatau River.

It was afternoon already, and great trees threw their shadows over the spot where she waited. She took hold of a hanging creeper and advanced another step. Then she saw something caught on a sharp rock, just at the creek's mouth. In the distance she heard a sound as of paddles in the stream. The sound was faint and soon faded.

Nyla almost lost her hold on the creeper. She could see a spirit raft of food caught on that rock, yet she could not believe her eyes. It couldn't possibly be real. She must already be haunted by the evil spirits of this place and was seeing objects that didn't exist. She shook herself. "No, I trust in God." She spoke the words aloud.

Strength entered into her, and she let the creeper go, waded out into the swift stream and laid hold of the raft laden with food. Then she realized what she was doing. This was a spirit raft. Some upriver village had set this raft of food adrift to turn aside some calamity. Perhaps her own village had launched it. This was a spirit raft for the use of spirits only, not for the relief of girls lost in jungle clearings with crocodiles and snakes.

Even while her mind was thinking these thoughts, her hands were busy guiding the raft into the creek, and her feet were finding firm places to step among the rocks beneath the surface of the swift water. If she should slip or fall she would surely lose the raft. She managed every step until she reached the roots that guarded the entrance of the crocodile's den, but she must not think about the crocodile now. She needed to give all her attention to bringing the raft to shore.

"I am not a spirit." Nyla made the announcement in a loud voice. She intended to warn all the spirits that she knew exactly what she was doing. "I am not a spirit, but I am very hungry, and I trust in God who is greater than all the spirits."

She listened. No answer came from the jungle—only the buzz of innumerable insects in the afternoon sunshine, and the sound of the forest birds as they called to one another from the green treetops.

She drew the raft from the water and carried every morsel of food to her *lankau*. It was not until every crumb had been carried up there that Nyla sat down to eat.

For all her great hunger, she did not eat greedily. She ate only enough to relieve the sharpest pangs of hunger. Also she ate the food that would spoil soonest. She saved the rest.

After such refreshment, she barred the door to her hut with lengths of thatch and sheets of woven leaves and lay down to sleep. She felt better than she had for days, and although the menace of the sleeping python in the bamboo worried her, she put it aside. When she wakened the following morning the sun was rising.

She went to the door of her *lankau,* removed the protection she had piled there the night before, and looked out into the bright morning. A great thankfulness rose up within her. Yes, Poojee was right. God is everywhere, and those who trust Him are always safe. She ran down to the creek to bathe and came back to eat of the delicious food prepared for the spirits.

A newborn love for God and an old fear of the spirits struggled in her mind. She knew that only a God who was everywhere, and who knew all things, could have sent Poojee to their village the day of the feast. Yet all the superstition of her tribe crowded up to battle with the new faith.

Again she gathered up her courage and went to the bamboo thicket to examine the snake. The bulge was not so large as yesterday, but it was still there. The creature would not waken today and probably not tomorrow. She went about her daily tasks with some pleasure.

She turned the bamboos that were curing in the creek. She even hacked at the sago trees with the intention of preparing some of the hated sago to stretch her food supply a few days longer.

So the days passed. Each morning Nyla went first to visit the python in the bamboo. Then, assured that he would not waken that day, she bathed and looked for the white crocodile. She had not seen the Great White One for several days now and wondered why.

Finally came a morning when Nyla gazed with chattering teeth. She could not see the slightest bulge in the smooth length of the great snake. Even as she looked she thought that the huge body seemed uneasy. Although the snake was still deeply drowsy, he was surely wakening.

She flew back to her *lankau,* and all the terror of her first fright of the snake came back and overwhelmed her.

Nyla almost fainted from fright. Then it seemed to her as though a calm hand was laid on her heart, and she remembered God. How could she forget? She sat on her mat and sang over and over again the words of Poojee's song:

>"'God is with me everywhere;
>I am safe, always safe.'"

Later in the afternoon she parted the thatch and looked out. The snake was awake! There was a stirring in the grass. A forest jay scolded overhead. A squirrel chattered and frisked through treetops. All the small forest creatures knew.

This was the day of the snake. She thought of the night she had come to this place, the dreadful night she had hung in the fire-spirit tree.

"I will go back to the tree," she cried out.

With great leaps she crossed the clearing and dashed for the trunk of the fire-spirit tree. The sun was almost down. She worked herself along the trunk over the river. Dreadful sounds came from the thicket behind her—mighty threshings and a terrible voice. It was the voice of a demon, Nyla was sure of that. Ah, how foolish she had been to eat the spirit food. No doubt it had been intended for the king of demons, and now he had roused himself in anger.

The noises grew louder. The girl reached the crotch of the tree where she had spent the night ten days ago. The hours wore on with intervals of silence broken now and then by horrible sounds from the bamboo.

Then Nyla heard another sound, a familiar sound—the dipping of paddles in the stream. A boat was coming from downriver, someone from the fort, perhaps. At the thought of people so close, she lifted her voice in a wail of anguish that sounded through the dark night with sharp echoes from the far banks of the stream.

She cried out again and again, but the only answer was a renewal of the hideous noises from the bamboo. The boat had vanished back down the river. And no wonder, Nyla thought, the sounds from this cursed sandbank were enough to scare away the bravest of warriors.

She ceased her crying and huddled in the friendly crotch of the tree. She knew exactly what was going to happen. Now that she had cried out, the python must know where she had hidden. He would come and seek her out, and then…

She slipped both arms through a loop of creeper that hung in the branching tree and balanced the upper part of her body in the swing it provided. Fearing that she might faint and fall, she swung herself there and waited for the morning.

11

CHIEF Ladah wakened early the morning after his quarrel with Malik. He hurried down to the river and bathed quickly, then stood for a few minutes on the wharf, shaking the water from his body and enjoying the sunshine as it warmed him and dried his long hair.

Even after he had twisted his hair into a long knot, he still hesitated to go back up to the longhouse. He knew that Malik was furious. Perhaps the witch doctor had not slept last night either. He might have spent the night making medicine against the teacher. Chief Ladah wondered whether spirit charms and devil medicine would harm Poojee.

The eddy that whirled in front of Ladah's wharf was not so strong now as it had been a few days ago, but still the current's circular motion caught small objects, leaves, twigs, and dead blossoms, and drifted them slowly around in a ring of floating rubbish.

Something in the tangle caught the chief's attention. He watched the object circle in closer and closer until he was able to reach out and poke it with a stick.

The object was the figure of a man rudely carved from soft wood and as long as his own forearm. It was a devil charm, and sure to bring dreadful calamity to anyone who touched it, as well as to the person it represented.

The figure was not naked. The crude carving suggested a

105

shirt and short pants and a sun helmet. No question about it, the figure looked like Poojee. The chief poked at it some more, turning it over with the stick and examining it. Then he saw the likeness of a small spear thrust into the figure's chest.

The chief shoved the devil charm out into the stream and watched it circle around and finally disappear down the river. Malik must have been up all night making this witch medicine. He wanted to get rid of the teacher and had decided to destroy him with charms. Everyone knew that such a figure, set adrift with the proper ceremonies and curses, was certain to cause the victim's death.

The chief resisted his first impulse to cry out and warn the whole village of what had happened and insist that Malik make his strongest witchcraft and remove the curse. A week ago he would have done just that. Now he waited and considered.

He knew that the village people had come to like Poojee and enjoy his stories and his songs. As for himself, his own heart was strongly taken with this new magic from the God who is everywhere. Poojee's magic was strong, probably stronger than any devil medicine, but here was a chance to prove it. If some evil or misfortune should come to Poojee, then he would know that the old customs were best, and that Malik was right.

Another thought came to him. After this he would see to it that Poojee's sleeping mat was inside the closed door of his own room. He would take no more chances by letting the teacher sleep on the inner veranda. If the curse was going to come because of the devil charm, then let it come; but the chief was determined that Malik should not do anything more.

Up in the longhouse veranda, Ladah heard singing. He knew that Poojee had gathered all the villagers to worship God with singing. The chief's heart lifted. He liked this new custom of welcoming the day with songs and worship to the unseen God. He climbed the ladder and took his place in the circle.

He looked around for Malik. The witchman had come. He sat among the others and looked as satisfied as a cat that has just robbed a fish trap. He watched the teacher closely.

Chief Ladah looked at Poojee's face bright with happiness, as he led the people through the songs. How could he know that he was marked for death? Or was he?

After the villagers had scattered to their bathing and their morning work, the chief spoke to Poojee. "It is now the fifth day since my daughter was taken. After today there is little hope that the men will find the crocodile. It is too long."

"Yes, I know." Poojee seemed to be thinking. "Come with me today, and we will cross the river to Sawa's village. I want to see how Sawa's wounded arm is healing."

As the chief and Poojee pulled out into the river, Chief Ladah could no longer control his eagerness. "Tell me, teacher," he asked, "can your God protect against devil charms?"

"People make such charms in my country, too." Poojee pulled strongly with the paddle. "Those who trust in God cannot be touched by such magic. God is stronger than all witchcraft and all curses."

Ladah settled himself comfortably in the prow of the boat and laid a strong hand to his paddle. In a short time they reached Chief Sawa's village.

They found the young chief under the longhouse, where he was directing two men who were making a big dugout from a single log. He came to meet them, and Ladah saw that his left arm and hand were wrapped in a neat covering of young banana leaf.

At sight of the teacher, Sawa stripped off the leaf covering and showed the teacher the bandaged hand just as Poojee had splinted it the evening of the feast day—clean and white.

"No one has touched it," Sawa said proudly as he clenched his good hand.

"Does it hurt?"

"Not much anymore."

"Well, don't let anyone touch it until I come to take the bandage off."

Chief Sawa smiled. "No one shall touch it."

Then Sawa turned to Chief Ladah. "Have the warriors found the crocodile who took your daughter?"

"Not yet," Ladah answered. "It is the fifth day, and no one has found anything. It is too long. I think they will not find her."

Disregarding the chief's words, Sawa spoke to Poojee. "They tell me that you came down from Sidang on the feast day to care for my broken wrist. Is that true?"

Poojee nodded.

"My people tell me that no one called you, that you heard the drums of your God. Is that true?"

"That is true," Poojee said. "The drums of God sound in our minds and warn us of danger or tell us what God wants us to do."

"I have been listening," Sawa said. "All the time, I listen for those drums. I hear them. Are you listening now?"

"What do you mean?" Poojee put his hand on the young chief's shoulder. "What do the drums of God say to you?"

"They say that the God you worship must like me. Otherwise why would He have called you to help me?"

"Oh, that is certainly true." Poojee patted Sawa on the

shoulder. "There is no question about that. God is very fond of you."

"Well, I don't know anything about God, except for what some of the people from Sidang's village have told me. I would like to know more." The young chief looked at the teacher and smiled. "Then I can listen better to God's drums. I want to hear them all the time."

Sawa led the way up into the longhouse and called his people together. Poojee told them the story of God's power and love.

When the stories and songs were finished, Sawa followed his visitors down to the wharf. As Poojee untied the chief's boat, Sawa said, "Isn't it strange that the drums of God have told you nothing about the chief's daughter? Doesn't God like Nyla and her father as much as He likes me?"

Poojee stood for a moment with his paddle in his hand, looking at Sawa with surprise on his face. "I shall listen better," the teacher said, and they shoved off into the river.

"What did he mean?" Ladah asked when they were out into the current of the stream. "He acts as though he knows something we don't."

"Perhaps he does." Poojee spoke in a serious tone. "Sometimes those who have known and loved God for a long time get dull ears, while those who have heard His voice only a few times listen so eagerly that they hear more."

All the way back to the village, Poojee seemed in deep thought, and when they reached the longhouse, the chief saw him take his little black book from his bundle. He sat for a long time on the outer veranda, looking at it.

Again that evening the crocodile hunters came back with no news. But one boatload of warriors had stopped at Tatau

Fort, the government post on the river, and they brought a letter for Poojee. They all gathered around to watch him open it. No letter had come into the village before, because, of course, no one could read.

"It is good news," Poojee said as he folded the letter and put it back into the envelope. "The government is giving a piece of fine, rich land where we can make a village for God's worship. It will be for everyone on this river and even other rivers."

"Where is it? Where is it?" Great excitement ran through the company.

"I am not quite sure. It says here," he looked again at the letter, "it says that the ground is on this side of the river, and in the curve of a stream called Batoo Creek. Do you know where that is?"

Yes, they all knew. It was down three bends of the river, not too far away, and about half the distance to Tatau Fort. Last year Malik had planted rice there, but the place was so full of evil spirits and bad birds that Malik had never harvested his crop, and no one had been back It was a cursed place. No Dyak would ever set foot on that ground in the curve of Batoo Creek.

"The men who will come to make the village for God will not be afraid of evil spirits or bad birds," Poojee told them. "You will see. The evil spirits will not stay where people love and worship God."

He explained that other teachers would come, and before long the village must be built. Long into the night they talked about it. So interested and eager were they, not one person thought to look to see whether the white crocodile had come back.

That night Chief Ladah insisted that Poojee move his mat inside the room where the chief's family lived.

"I am not afraid," Poojee told him.

"Of evil spirits, I am no longer afraid," the chief said. "But of evil men, I am afraid. We must be watchful and try not to have trouble with them."

Poojee laughed and moved his mat in beside Chief Ladah's.

No one saw the stealthy figure that crept down the inner veranda late in the night. No one saw the rays of the rising moon flash on the knife blade, and no one saw the knife that hovered over an empty place where a man had slept last night and the night before.

No one saw. But someone heard the muffled curses and the hissing breath. Chief Ladah turned on his mat, then sat up and strained his ears to catch the deadly sounds. He did not need to see.

Next day all the visiting warriors, who had spent five days scouring the river for the killer crocodile, met with all the men of Ladah's longhouse in a last council session. They all agreed that there was no longer any hope of catching the guilty crocodile. Some thought they had not been watchful enough and the creature had escaped them. Most of them believed that evil spirits had snatched Nyla away without leaving a trace.

With grateful words, the chief thanked them all and dismissed them. One by one, they untied their boats and scattered up and down the river to their own longhouses. In the late afternoon the chief sent three of his own men down to Tatau Fort to get salt and oil, for the many visitors had used up all the village supplies.

When late evening came and the men had not returned, the chief supposed that they had decided to spend the night at the fort and would come back in the morning.

Just before daybreak, a great tumult arose below the village at the log wharf. The chief and Poojee leaped down the notched log, and all the other village people tumbled out in great fright to find out what terrible thing could have happened now. The men who had gone to the fort climbed out of their boat so shaken with terror that it was impossible to get any understandable word out of them.

Finally, after the chief had counted them and looked them over and made sure that none of them were hurt, he took them up into the longhouse veranda and commanded the women to light lamps and set food and drink before them. At last one of the men recovered enough to tell the story.

"We left the fort late," he began. "The ride was running in, so we expected to have a fine trip. We paddled along the river until we came near the curve where Batoo Creek flows into the river." The man trembled as though with a chill. "You know we usually cross the river and go by on the other side, on account of the evil spirits; but we remembered the letter the teacher got yesterday and what he said about the new village for God that will be built there, so we decided to go close to it and have a look."

Again the man shuddered and shook, and his teeth chattered with fright; but the chief soothed him and in a moment he was able to go on. Malik came and sat by the men and watched them out of his small eager eyes.

"What a foolish thing to do," Malik said. "There is a heavy curse on that spot, and crowds of evil spirits live at the entrance of Batoo Creek."

"Yes." The man took up his story again. "We found that out. We were still some distance down the river when we heard a terrible fight going on among the evil spirits, also we heard a great and terrible voice from the shore—the voice of the great serpent, the king of the swampland. He cried out again and again. I wanted to turn back, but the others said it was only a snake, so we paddled a little closer and then——"

The man's eyes rolled back in his head and such a fit of violent shaking seized him that he could say nothing more.

The chief turned to the other two men. "Tell us, what happened?" Chief Ladah was angry. "You are not hurt. You are here, safe in our longhouse. What are you, anyway, fools, or cowards, or both?"

One of the men spoke up. "We heard another voice answering the great snake. We knew whose voice it was—the voice of Nyla, the chief's daughter."

Every person in the veranda was struck dumb. For a moment, Chief Ladah felt as though he had been pierced through the heart by a poisoned dart. He looked around the dimly lighted circle and deathly fear sat on every face. Even Malik writhed and gasped, but no words came from his lips.

Poojee spoke first. He jumped to his feet and cried out in a loud voice, "Come, let us go!"

Everyone in the circle stared at him as though he had gone mad.

"We must go, men. Get your paddles." He hurried to bring his paddle.

"Wait," the chief commanded. "You must not go. My daughter is dead. Don't you know that? She is dead and her spirit is crying out there in the night with the great snake."

Poojee came back and stood before the chief. "Your daughter is not dead. She is alive. She is alone there in the curve of Batoo Creek. She has been there for ten days."

113

Chief Sawa stuck his head up at the top of the ladder. "I have come," he said. Poojee asked in surprise, "You hear them too—the drums?" "I heard them."

Ladah sprang up. "How can you say such things? It cannot be true. It cannot be true!"

Then the teacher looked around on all the people and smiled. "The drums of God are telling me," he said. "If I had listened well, they would have told me sooner, four days ago."

Poojee stood waiting. "Are none of you coming with me? Must I go alone?" He looked at Chief Ladah, then down at the river where the first flush of new day lay along the murky water.

At that moment a voice called from the wharf and everyone sitting on the veranda started and cried out as though struck a violent blow. A moment later Chief Sawa stuck his head up at the top of the ladder. His face shone with joy. He came on up and stood among them with his bandaged hand across his stomach, and he smiled down at the circle of frightened faces.

"I have come," he said. "Two of my men are down there in my dugout. We are ready."

Then Poojee came with the paddle in his hand and touched Sawa's good arm. "You heard them too—the drums?"

"I heard them."

Chief Ladah jumped to his feet, then ran for his paddle, and the three of them left; while every mouth in the circle of faces gaped, and every eye bulged with fear and surprise.

Sawa's boat was large and roomy. Without a word the men bent their paddles in strong determined strokes—all but Sawa who sat in the center of the dugout and fixed his eyes on the river ahead.

As the light strengthened, the boat shot forward around the first curve below the village, around the next one. And at the third bend, the men pulled in toward the sandbar at the mouth of Batoo Creek. It was then they saw Malik careening down after them, alone in his light dugout. He raced madly past them and thrust his canoe up on the sand of the cursed ground.

(Before we learn what Malik did next, we must go back to see how Nyla fared during the night and what she did first thing in the morning.)

12

TO Nyla, swinging in the loop of vine in the fire-spirit tree, the day seemed long in coming. The season of the tiny blooming flowers was over now, and no small fire-spirits came with their tiny torches. The flood of heavy rain that had scoured all the banks of Tatau River had thundered and tumbled its way to the ocean. The stream lay quiet.

The night would have been pleasant and ordinary except for two things: Nyla was all alone in a tree beside the cursed sandbank, and she had been in this lonely spot for ten days. Also, in the bamboo behind her, a fierce struggle raged. The mighty swamp python thrashed, twisted, and floundered with bursting noises as the joints of the bamboo shattered or exploded. The crashing tumult was mixed with the horrid voice of the enormous snake—a high-pitched whistling cry fit to paralyze any creature with fright.

When late the evening before, Nyla heard paddles in the river and cried out in sudden hope, she realized that she had not only revealed her hiding place to the snake, but that the people in the boat, whoever they were, must have been badly scared. And who could blame them? The boat had slipped silently away without another sound.

With deeper discouragement than she had yet known, the girl fastened herself in the loop of tough vine that swung from the tree branches, and waited, expecting every moment to hear the scaly python trailing her along the slanted tree trunk.

But time passed. The sounds from the bamboo broke out from time to time, always with the noise of the terrible crunching and thrashing of a heavy body mingled with the weird cries of the big snake, but the noises did not come closer. They came always from the same place. At last Nyla was sure that the snake must be caught in the tangle of tough bamboo, and she remembered how the new growth of bamboo shoots had laced back and forth over the sleeping python. Could the bamboo be stronger than the huge snake? It must be so.

Gradually her heartbeat quieted. Her breath came naturally, and thoughts of home, of father and mother and little Djeelee, filled her mind. She thought of Poojee and his song, of the God whom Poojee worshiped. She remembered how the teacher had come to their village—oh, very long ago, it seemed to her now—and brought help for Chief Sawa when his wrist was broken on the day of the feast The "drums of God" had called him, he said, and he had come.

Then Nyla prayed the second prayer of her life:

"O God of the teacher Poojee, beat all Your drums so that someone will hear and come for me."

She wondered, after she had prayed, who would hear such drums, for she knew they must be heard in the heart and mind and not with the ear. How could the heart's ear be opened? Who could catch such sounds in the mind? Of course, Poojee could. He had heard once and he could hear again. One person was enough; one person could lead a whole village to the curve of Batoo Creek.

Encouraged and comforted, the girl drowsed, and when she wakened the light was rising in the east. The cool breeze that followed the tide lifted her hair and caressed her face. She looked toward the clump of bamboo, but she could hear no sound, no voice.

Her fear was gone. God, who could use the green fingers of the bamboo to imprison the great snake, could do anything; and she felt sure now that God had sent her the food on the spirit raft. She had almost decided to climb down from the tree and go back to her lankau when she heard the quick dip of paddles in the river. A boat was coming down on the near side of the stream. No, two boats were coming. The irregular beat of the paddles told her there were two. She loosened herself from the creeper and climbed out on the tree branch so far that it bent with her weight. Now she could see the first boat as it shot out of the shadows at the curve just above Batoo Creek.

She put all her strength into a single wild cry of joy that could be heard even to the second bend of the river. Every man in the first boat raised his head and she recognized her father, the teacher, and then young Chief Sawa sitting in the middle of the dugout with his bandaged hand across his chest and a look of brightness on his face.

In that instant it was her father's face that took all her attention. When he lifted his head at her cry, it was as though all the light of the new morning had gathered and burst into fire on his handsome face.

She hardly noticed Malik's little canoe as it came down with wild speed onto the sand bar.

Sawa's dugout darted under the tree, and the next instant Nyla was in her father's arms. No word was spoken, but the drawn breath from every throat was a sigh of great content; and it seemed to Nyla as though the whole forest, the river, and the sky rushed together in a surge of relief and delight.

Sawa's dugout darted under the tree, and the next instant Nyla was in her father's arms. It seemed to Nyla that the whole forest, the river, and the sky surged with relief and delight.

Then a fierce tumult broke out again in the bamboo thicket. Nyla drew away from her father. "It is the great snake; he slept in the bamboo, and now it will not let him go."

Quickly the rowers tied their canoe to the shore. Malik was first on the sandbank, and with hurried incantations he removed the taboo sign he had planted there months ago. Then all the men climbed out of the boat and went to look at the snake. Nyla followed them.

Seeing that the python was trapped among the tough bamboo shoots and could not possibly get away, a mighty courage entered into Malik and he led the attack. They all fell on the snake with their spears and put an abrupt end to its difficulties. Then they began to cut the dead reptile into lengths. No delicacy was more acceptable to the Dyaks than fresh snake meat, and here was plenty for two villages.

For one who had been hounded from this spot by bad birds and evil omens, Malik made rather free in his old rice field. He went to look at his old *lankau,* which Nyla had repaired. He inspected the thatching job, kicked at the empty shells of the penang palm stump where Nyla had clawed out the fat grubs. He picked up the knife, now sharp and shiny, and examined it. Last of all, he discovered the bamboo raft that had held the spirit food. He did not touch it, but squatted on the ground beside it and studied it as though he could read its story.

Finally Malik came back to the sand bar where the men were cutting up the snake, and he helped them load the lengths of meat into the dugouts. They piled it in both boats, distributing the weight evenly, for the python was long and very heavy.

As they still stood on the bank a ripple in the water at the mouth of the creek drew everyone's attention. The white crocodile swam into the mouth of the little stream, pushed down between the tree roots, and disappeared.

"So that explains it," Malik said, as though much relieved.

"Explains what?" Chief Sawa asked.

"The white crocodile has her den here at the mouth of Batoo Creek, and that is why she pushed the spirit raft down here. Of course, it was easy for Nyla to get it."

"Do you think so?" Poojee smiled at the witch doctor.

"She dared to eat of the food that was offered to evil spirits." Malik spoke more in wonder than in blame. "How could she do that?"

"I was so hungry," Nyla said. "I remembered that Poojee had told us about God—how God is stronger than all the crocodiles and all the curses in the world. So I dared to eat."

Then Nyla remembered her prayer in the tree. She turned to the other men. "Did you hear the drums?"

"We heard," Sawa told her, and Nyla's mind was filled with a new wonder. Had Sawa come to believe in God too?

"Poojee and I both heard the drums." Sawa smiled to see her surprise.

Malik looked at all of them as though they were talking nonsense. "Nyla had no drums here. How could any of you hear drums?"

Chief Ladah and Nyla chose to ride back to the village with Malik, while Poojee came with Sawa and his men.

When the boats rounded the curve below Ladah's village, Nyla could see that the log wharf was crowded with the village people. Everyone in the longhouse must be there, but her eyes picked out the two she wanted most to look at—her mother and her brother, Djeelee.

As the two boats drew near enough for the people on the

wharf to see, Nyla stood up in the dugout. A cry of fearful wonder went up from the whole company, and a moment later Nyla was in her mother's arms.

They all went up into the longhouse, and Nyla heard Poojee and Chief Sawa talking.

"It is a great wonder to me," Poojee was saying. "Yet I don't know why it should be. God can use a crocodile as well as a raven."

"What do you mean?" Sawa asked as the other villagers pressed close to hear.

"There is a beautiful story in the Book of God about a good man who was alone by a creek, something like Batoo Creek, I suppose, and he had no food. So God sent ravens with food for him every morning and every evening. There were many ravens in that country, and I suppose that is why God used them; but of course, He could use crocodiles just as easily."

Then Poojee explained to all of them how he had followed the white crocodile to the mouth of Batoo Creek on the day the village people had launched the raft of food—the third day after she came to beg for an offering. "I was very dull that day." He shook his head. "I should have known then that Nyla was there in the curve of Batoo Creek, but I was not listening well."

Chief Ladah sat with his daughter by his side and told all the people how the God who is everywhere had taken care of Nyla on the cursed land; and how God had fenced in the python, which might have eaten her, with the bamboo shoots.

Malik sat among them, but he made only one comment "That white crocodile has a den at the mouth of Batoo Creek."

"Then she isn't a spirit crocodile," one of the village men said. "She must be an ordinary crocodile just like the others."

Nyla sat in the circle and told how she had been trapped under the big floating log and carried away down three bends of the river, and how she had saved herself by clinging to the fire-spirit tree. She told how she had spent ten days in Malik's old rice field, how she had found the raft carrying the spirit food, and eaten the delicacies. "And now I know that Poojee speaks the truth. God is everywhere. He saved me on the cursed ground. He is greater than our fears."

Sawa spoke too. He held up his bandaged wrist for all to see. "The living God, who is everywhere, saved my hand. He called the teacher, Poojee, at the right moment and while I was drunk and helpless. I know that He cares for me, and from this time forward I will worship only God."

So the power of the evil spirits was challenged among the longhouses of Tatau River, and a few weeks later, as Poojee had told them, a new village sprang up in the curve of Batoo Creek.

Months went by, and a school stood where Nyla's little *lankau* hut had been. Close to it a house of worship lifted clean new walls and a peaked roof to the clear tropical sky, and on a rise of the hill behind the fire-spirit tree a medicine house opened its doors and offered help to all the sick people in the river villages.

More teachers came, and the light of the gospel of God shone through the darkness on Tatau River, driving out the cruel superstitions that had held the people in fear so many years.

Nyla was one of the first girls to attend the school, and she learned to read and write and sing and sew and all the other things schoolgirls learn in every country. Later, her little brother, Djeelee, came to school too, and so did Chief Sawa's children.

Among the people who lingered about the school and the medicine house, Malik, the witch doctor, spent the most time and seemed the most curious. Little by little, he began to admit that the magic of God was stronger and better than his own.

One evening after the school had been going for months, Nyla sat on the outer veranda of Ladah's longhouse reading the New Testament. The sunset spread its colors over the northern mountains and gleamed across the river's calm surface, for it was the turn of the tide. Nothing disturbed the calm stillness or marred the beauty of the scene. Then the girl heard a slight sound and ran to the veranda railing. The white crocodile was coming into the creek below the village.

Nyla did not raise her voice or call anyone to come and look, because no one cared how often the crocodile came. No one feared the creature any more. And the perfect peace of the fading day came down to meet the perfect peace in Nyla's heart.

Author's Note

I wanted to write this story a long time before I did. I wanted to show the wild beauty of Borneo's deep jungle, the cruel superstition that meets the Christian teacher, and the courage that such a teacher must have to carry the gospel to such a place.

I also wanted to show the river in its tumult at floodtime and its tranquil peace at the turn of the tide. And I wanted to show the crocodile. The crocodile did not only the things recorded in this story but many others so fantastic that I am afraid no one would believe them if I wrote them down.

The python was caught in the clump of bamboos where today the Seventh-day Adventist mission maintains an active program. The Bukit Nyala school has an enrollment of about a hundred boys and girls. A new church stands on the same grounds, and a modern airstrip provides for regular visits of the mission plane (The Angel).

I helped trim up that bamboo thicket a year or so after the python incident. The crocodile came to beg food while my husband was staying in the village. He saw it and was as puzzled as Poojee in the story.

Perhaps the white crocodile still lives in her den at the mouth of Batoo Creek. (Crocodiles are characteristically long-lived.) No one would think of doing the creature any harm.

Nyla's father came to the United States for a short visit in 1968. He appeared on several TV broadcasts, and millions of people heard from him much of what I have recounted in this book. He told how he became a Christian and helped to build the school on the banks of the very river where so much of the content of this story took place.